Collection Two

CLEMENTINE ROSE

Books by Jacqueline Harvey

Collection Two

CLEMENTINE ROSE

Jacqueline Harvey

RANDOM HOUSE AUSTRALIA

A Random House book
Published by Penguin Random House Australia Pty Ltd
Level 3, 100 Pacific Highway, North Sydney NSW 2060
www.penguin.com.au

Penguin
Random House
Australia

Clementine Rose and the Farm Fiasco first published by
Random House Australia in 2013
Clementine Rose and the Seaside Escape first published by
Random House Australia in 2014
Clementine Rose and the Treasure Box first published by
Random House Australia in 2014
This omnibus edition first published by Random House Australia in 2017

Addresses for the Penguin Random House group of companies can be
found at global.penguinrandomhouse.com/offices.

National Library of Australia
Cataloguing-in-Publication entry

Author: Harvey, Jacqueline
Title: Clementine Rose: collection two/Jacqueline Harvey
ISBN: 978 0 14378 865 2 (pbk)
Series: Harvey, Jacqueline. Clementine Rose.
Target audience: For primary school age
Subjects: Girls – Juvenile fiction

Cover and internal illustrations by J.Yi
Cover design by Leanne Beattie
Internal design by Midland Typesetters
Typeset in ITC Century 12.5/19 by Midland Typesetters, Australia
Printed in Australia by Griffin Press, an accredited ISO AS/NZS
14001:2004 Environmental Management System printer

Penguin Random House Australia uses papers that are natural,
renewable and recyclable products and made from wood grown
in sustainable forests. The logging and manufacturing processes
are expected to conform to the environmental regulations of the
country of origin.

CLEMENTINE ROSE
and the Farm Fiasco

Jacqueline Harvey

RANDOM HOUSE AUSTRALIA

For Darcy, Flynn and Eden,
and for Ian, the best 'manager'
anyone could ever wish for

CRACK!

Clementine Rose gripped her pencil and stared at the page. Mrs Bottomley said that they should try to spell a word before asking for help. Clementine thought for a moment. Then, as neatly as she could, she wrote the letters *h-a-t-c-h*.

Mrs Bottomley was walking around the room inspecting everyone's work. She stopped beside Clementine's desk and squinted through her glasses.

'Let me see what you've got there, Clementine. *The egg is going to hatch*. Where did you copy that from?'

Clementine shook her head. 'I didn't. I wrote it myself.'

Mrs Bottomley's forehead puckered. 'Come now, Clementine. Perhaps Astrid might have helped you?' She smiled at the girl sitting behind Clemmie.

Clementine looked up at her teacher. 'No, Mrs Bottomley. I sounded it out by myself.'

'If you say so,' the teacher replied, pursing her lips.

Clementine frowned. She wondered why Mrs Bottomley didn't believe her. 'May I go and see if anything's happening?' she asked.

'Happening?' Mrs Bottomley repeated. 'Where?'

Clementine pointed. 'Over there.' Mrs Bottomley wasn't very good at remembering things sometimes.

'I think you should draw a picture first, and then you can have a look – although I don't imagine anything will have changed in the last few minutes.'

Clementine began to draw her illustration at the bottom of the page. She was trying to imagine what the chick would look like. She thought it would be fluffy and yellow, like the picture of a chick that was stuck up on the back wall.

Mrs Bottomley disappeared into the store-room. Clementine stood up and walked towards the incubator. It had been set up on a table at the back of the room by Poppy's father, Mr Bauer. It had glass sides and glaring lamps, and eight creamy eggs sitting inside.

'Come on, little chickens,' she whispered. 'Please come out soon.'

The eggs sat perfectly still.

Clementine hadn't noticed Angus standing behind her.

'I'm going to eat those eggs for breakfast tomorrow,' he said.

Clementine spun around. 'No, you can't! They're not breakfast eggs, they're chick eggs.'

'They're boring eggs,' Angus sneered. 'They don't do anything.'

While Angus babbled on about his mother making an omelette, something caught Clementine's attention.

She put her finger to her lips. 'Shh! Look!'

'There's nothing hap–' The boy stopped suddenly. 'It just moved.'

Clementine and Angus watched as one of the little eggs rocked from side to side. They peered closer and then looked at each other and smiled.

'Something's coming out!' Angus exclaimed.

'Angus, Clementine, neither of you have finished your work,' said Mrs Bottomley as she emerged from the storeroom. 'I said that you could look at the eggs once your drawings were done.'

'Mrs Bottomley,' Clementine called. 'One of the eggs is moving.'

The whole class stopped what they were doing and looked around.

'Cool,' said Joshua. He slid out of his seat and raced over.

'Joshua Tribble, go back to your desk,' Mrs Bottomley directed.

Clementine and Angus hadn't moved. Their eyes were glued to the glass case.

'There's a beak, there's a beak!' Clementine shouted.

The rest of the class ran towards the incubator.

'Sit down at once.' Mrs Bottomley's voice boomed, but she didn't stand a chance against a mob of excited five-year-olds.

The head teacher, Miss Critchley, happened to be passing the classroom and looked in to see the children rushing around like a swarm of bees.

'What's going on in here?' she asked cheerfully as she strode into the room.

'Children, sit down!' Mrs Bottomley demanded.

'Miss Critchley, there's a beak,' Clementine shouted above the din.

'All right, everyone, settle down.' Miss Critchley's voice was like honey. The children stopped their shouting at once. 'You don't want to frighten the chick, do you? Gather around. If you're in the front, please kneel down so the people behind you can see.'

Mrs Bottomley harrumphed loudly and moved in behind Joshua.

The whole class was transfixed as the little egg shook and the tip of a beak broke through again.

'It needs my dad's saw,' Joshua said.

'I think it's doing a wonderful job with its beak,' said Miss Critchley, smiling. The little hole was spreading out to become a line around the middle of the egg.

'As if a chicken would have a saw inside an egg. That's stupid,' said Angus.

Joshua poked out his tongue. '*You're* stu–'

Miss Critchley interrupted the lads. 'There'll be no name-calling, thank you, boys. Let's just see what happens.'

The children watched as the chick made

more cracks in the shell. They oohed and aahed as the tiny creature began to break free.

'This is boring,' Joshua complained. 'How long does it take to get out of an egg?'

'You could sit down and do your work,' Mrs Bottomley suggested.

'That's more boring,' said Joshua.

There was a loud gasp as the egg finally broke in two and a wet chick wobbled to its feet.

'It's brown,' Angus said, clearly surprised.

'Like Mrs Bottomley.' Joshua laughed and turned around to look at his teacher. She was dressed in her usual uniform of brown shoes, brown stockings and a brown suit.

Clementine bit back a smile. She couldn't remember seeing her teacher wear any other colour.

Mrs Bottomley simply raised her eyebrows and the grin slid from Joshua's face.

'Do you think the other chicks will hatch soon?' Clementine asked.

Miss Critchley nodded. 'Yes, they shouldn't be too far behind.'

'Will we be able to hold them?' Sophie asked.

'You have to be careful,' said Poppy, 'because they can get cold.'

Everyone knew that Poppy was an authority on animals, as she lived on a farm.

'I'm gonna hold it first,' Angus declared. 'I saw it first.'

Astrid stared at the boy. 'Clemmie saw it first. She should have first hold.'

'Yes, I think that sounds fair,' said Miss Critchley. She winked at Clementine.

'Angus can go first if he wants to,' Clementine said.

The boy shrugged. 'It's okay, you can go.'

Clementine smiled. Sometimes it was hard to believe that Angus was the same boy who had been so horrible to her at the start of the year.

'I think we should give the chick a little while to get used to its surroundings,' said Miss Critchley. 'Why don't you all head back to your desks and I'll come around and have a look at your work.'

The children sped to their seats, eager to show their writing to the head teacher.

'Mrs Bottomley, do you have any stickers?' Miss Critchley asked.

Ethel Bottomley had a very large collection of stickers in the bottom of her desk drawer, but she used them sparingly.

'I suppose you could have these.' She pulled out a flat page of silver stars. The corners were slightly dog-eared.

Miss Critchley walked through the room admiring the children's work and sprinkling each page with stars, much to Mrs Bottomley's displeasure.

When she reached Clementine, Miss Critchley congratulated her on her efforts and suggested they sneak over to the incubator to see how the chick was getting on.

Clementine's eyes widened as she looked at the little bird. 'It's fluffy!'

'And I think it's about to get a new friend.' Miss Critchley pointed at another egg that was rocking gently. 'Would you like to hold the chick now?'

Clementine nodded. She'd never held a newly hatched chick before.

Miss Critchley reached in and gently picked up the baby. She told Clementine to hold her hands open and then placed the chick inside.

'It's so soft.' Clementine's smile was wide and her eyes sparkled.

'What do you think we should call him or her?' Miss Critchley asked.

Clementine thought hard. 'I think it's a girl. Her feathers feel like the velvet material Mrs Mogg used to make me a winter dress. Could we call her Velvet?'

'I think that's perfect, Clemmie,' Miss Critchley declared. 'Hello Velvet.'

An Exciting Announcement

By the end of the school day, three more chicks had hatched. Velvet had been joined by Lemonade, named by Angus, Henny Penny, named by Astrid, and Joshua, who'd been named by the boy himself.

Clementine wondered if all eight chicks would be there when they arrived for school the next morning.

'Hurry along, everyone. Pack your readers into your bags and come and sit on the floor. I have a notice for you to take home today,' Mrs Bottomley instructed.

Clementine wondered what the notice was about. The last one had said there was an outbreak of head lice. Her mother had inspected her hair and even washed it in some special shampoo to be sure. Clementine didn't like the thought of those creatures at all. She scratched her head.

Joshua looked at her. 'Have you got nits?'

'No.' Clementine's face turned red.

'Joshua Tribble, stop talking and hurry along,' Mrs Bottomley barked.

The children quickly found a place on the floor in front of Mrs Bottomley's special chair. No one was allowed to sit on it except her.

'I have some news but it's nothing to get too excited about,' Mrs Bottomley said sternly.

Sophie and Clementine looked at each other in bewilderment. Poppy smiled.

'I don't believe for one second that this is a good idea, but I've been overruled. Miss Critchley has arranged for us to visit the farm at Highton Hall on Friday.'

A cheer went up around the room.

'Shh. Stop that nonsense immediately or I'll leave you behind on Friday to do yard duty with Mr Pickles.' The teacher's face was red and she was huffing and blowing like a steam train.

Clementine leaned around and grinned at Poppy, who beamed back.

'Did you know?' Clemmie asked.

Poppy nodded. 'Daddy said that I couldn't tell because it wasn't definite, but now it must be.'

'I love farms,' Joshua said.

'Yes, well, I don't,' Mrs Bottomley said through gritted teeth. Before she could say any more, the bell rang for the end of the school day.

The kindergarten children cheered once more, picked up their bags, and streamed out of the classroom.

'Kindergarten! Two straight lines. Now!' Mrs Bottomley called after them but the children had scattered like Mexican jumping beans.

Miss Critchley was already standing at the school gate, where she liked to farewell the students each afternoon.

'We're going to Poppy's farm, Miss Critchley,' Clementine shouted as she raced towards her.

'It's a proper 'scursion, on a bus,' Angus called after her.

'You're going to have a wonderful time,' Miss Critchley told the children. She didn't add her next thought: *Even if Mrs Bottomley came up with every excuse under the sun not to take you.*

Mrs Bottomley appeared, muttering something under her breath.

'It's lovely to see the children so excited,' said Miss Critchley.

'Yes, I suppose you'd think it is.' Mrs Bottomley's lip curled and she marched off towards the staff room.

A WILD RIDE

Clementine stood at the gate and looked for Uncle Digby's ancient Mini Minor. She couldn't see it anywhere. Her tummy began to feel funny. It wasn't like him to be late.

'Don't worry, Clementine,' said Miss Critchley. 'I'm sure someone will be here to pick you up soon. If not, you can come and wait in my office.'

Clementine smiled back at the head teacher. Miss Critchley always knew the right thing to say.

A few minutes later, Aunt Violet's shiny red car roared down the road and skidded to a halt outside the school gates.

The old woman put down the passenger side window and leaned across. 'Don't just stand there, Clementine,' she called. 'I haven't got all day.'

'I didn't know you were coming to get me this afternoon,' said Clementine as she walked towards the car.

Miss Critchley followed. She opened the back door for Clementine and leaned inside. 'Hello Miss Appleby. Thank you for picking Clementine up, but I really must insist that you observe the speed limit outside the school.'

'Oh, I can see those signs perfectly well, Miss Critchley,' Aunt Violet replied. 'It's just that I was running late and I didn't want Clementine to worry.'

Clementine was surprised to hear this.

'We'd worry a lot more if you had an accident,' Miss Critchley insisted.

'I've never had an accident in my life and

I don't plan to start now,' the old woman retorted. 'If you'd remove yourself and allow Clementine to get settled, we'll be on our way.'

Clementine hopped into the back seat and buckled her seatbelt.

'Bossy woman,' Aunt Violet muttered. 'Who does she think she is?'

'She's the head teacher, of course,' Clementine piped up, wondering why Aunt Violet had asked.

'I don't care who she is, she needn't tell me how to drive.' Aunt Violet's face furrowed into a deep frown and she pulled out from the kerb sharply. There was a blast of a horn and a screech of brakes as Joshua Tribble's father only just managed to swerve and avoid hitting the side of the car.

Aunt Violet put down the window and yelled, 'What do you think you're doing, man? You could have killed us driving like that.'

'Excuse me, lady, but you pulled out and didn't even look,' Mr Tribble yelled back.

Joshua was sitting in the passenger seat.

He pulled on his cheeks and made a monster face at Clementine.

'Why don't you control your little brat?' Aunt Violet gave Joshua a scary stare.

The boy reeled in fright and covered his eyes.

Aunt Violet harrumphed loudly, then squeezed her car through the gap and sped off.

'Where's Mummy and Uncle Digby?' Clementine asked. She was beginning to hope that Aunt Violet wouldn't pick her up too often.

'They're talking to some builders about the roof,' Aunt Violet replied. 'And not before time.'

Clementine nodded and then remembered her news. She bounced in her seat. 'We're going on an excursion!'

'Yes, lovely,' Aunt Violet said absently.

'To Poppy's farm,' Clementine went on.

'It's not Poppy's farm, Clementine. It's the Highton-Smith-Kennington-Joneses',' her great-aunt replied.

Clementine didn't know what she meant. 'But Poppy lives there.'

'Yes, because her father and mother work there,' said Aunt Violet. 'But it's not theirs.'

'Oh,' Clementine said. It didn't matter who owned it. She was just excited that the whole class was going. 'Well, we're visiting on Friday. We're going to see horses and cows and sheep and chickens. And four of our chicks hatched in class today and I got to hold the first one and give her a name. She's called Velvet.'

'Vel–' Aunt Violet began. 'Not Violet?' She glanced in the rear-vision mirror and saw Clementine frown.

'No! That's your name. Her name is Velvet,' Clementine repeated. Sometimes Aunt Violet could be so silly. 'She's brown and fluffy and her feathers feel like my velvet dress.'

Her great-aunt simply nodded.

Aunt Violet turned the car into the driveway at Penberthy House and came to a halt outside the front door. Clementine scrambled out of her seatbelt, grabbed her schoolbag and jumped out of the car, slamming the door.

'Clementine!' Aunt Violet admonished. 'I'd

like that door to remain attached to the car, thank you very much.'

'Sorry, Aunt Violet!' Clementine called back. 'Thank you for coming to get me.' She skittered up the front steps and into the house.

Violet Appleby watched as Clementine disappeared. She wondered if the child had ever been more excited about anything in her life.

A THORNY CHAT

Clementine was counting down the days to Friday. Her mother and Uncle Digby thought the excursion was a wonderful idea, and Lady Clarissa immediately signed up to help. Two other parents had volunteered to come along and assist, and of course Mr and Mrs Bauer would be at the farm too.

On Thursday afternoon, Clementine was playing in the garden at home with Lavender. 'All of the eggs have hatched now and the chicks are so sweet. They've all got names too. You already know about Velvet, Lemonade, Henny Penny and Joshua, and now there's Blackie, Chicka, Hattie and Noodle,' she babbled to the little pig. 'Mrs Bottomley doesn't seem to like the names much, and she's giving us *so* many strange lessons about our visit to Poppy's farm. We're not to get too close to the animals; we have to wash our hands after touching any animals, which is silly because I touch you all the time.' Lavender snuffled indignantly and Clementine shook her head. 'And we mustn't pick anything to eat from the garden. But isn't that what a farm is for?'

Clementine tucked a daisy behind her ear and put one behind Lavender's ear as well. 'We're going to see cows and sheep and horses and I think there could even be some pigs too. But they won't be little teacup piggies like you. Mr Bauer has great big pigs. They have chickens and ducks as well. I can't wait. Mummy's coming and I wish we could take you, but you might get lost and that would be terrible. So you have to stay here with Uncle Digby and Aunt Violet and Pharaoh.'

Clementine was admiring the new buds on her mother's favourite rosebush when she heard a loud snipping sound behind her.

'Who are you talking to, Clementine?' Aunt Violet demanded. She'd just cut a long red rose and was in the process of removing the thorns.

'Oh, hello Aunt Violet, I was just telling Lavender all about the excursion tomorrow and explaining why she can't come.'

'And do you really think the pig understands you?' her great-aunt asked as she hacked another stem.

Clementine nodded. 'Yes, of course.'

'What a lot of drivel,' Aunt Violet snorted. 'She's a pig, for heaven's sake.'

'And pigs are really smart,' Clementine replied, wrinkling her nose.

'Here, hold these.' Aunt Violet passed Clementine the roses. The child hesitated. 'It's all right. I've taken the thorns off.'

'What are they for?' Clementine buried her nose in the centre of one of the flowers. 'They smell lovely.'

'They're for my room,' Violet replied. 'It could do with some cheering up.'

'Is it sad?' Clementine asked.

The old woman looked at Clementine. 'What are you talking about this time?'

'You said that your room could do with some cheering up so I thought it must be sad,' Clementine explained.

'I just want some roses to brighten the place up. Is that all right with you?' Aunt Violet cut three more blooms.

Clementine wondered why Aunt Violet was in a bad mood this time. 'Are you sad, Aunt Violet?'

'What?'

'Are you sad?' Clementine asked again. 'Are the flowers really to cheer you up?'

'You can think whatever you like, Clementine.' Aunt Violet snatched the roses and stalked off.

Clementine watched as Aunt Violet stomped through the garden, up the back steps and into the kitchen. She waited a little while then followed. Lavender snuffled along in the grass close behind her.

In the kitchen, Uncle Digby was cutting up some apples for a pie and Clemmie's mother was stirring something on the stovetop. She looked up as Clementine entered. 'Hello Clemmie, would you like a glass of milk and some afternoon tea?'

'Yes, please.'

'I left you something to eat,' Uncle Digby said. There was half a chocolate eclair sitting underneath the cake dome.

'Yum,' the child squealed.

'The doctor said that I have to go easy on the sweet treats,' said Uncle Digby. He patted his chest above his heart. 'So I'm sharing with you.'

Clementine nodded. She didn't want Uncle Digby to have any more scares like the one he'd had a little while ago, when they'd been hosting a wedding at the house.

'Where's Aunt Violet?' she enquired.

'Oh, I don't know. I heard her come in and she hurried away upstairs. I hope she's not coming down with another one of her headaches,' said Lady Clarissa, sighing.

Digby raised his eyebrows. 'Yes, we all know what that means.'

'She can't help it if she gets nasty headaches,' Lady Clarissa told the old man.

'Did you say she can't help it if she has a nasty head?' Digby chuckled. Clementine giggled too.

'Digby Pertwhistle, you cheeky thing,' Clarissa admonished. 'I think there has been some steady improvement in Aunt Violet's behaviour recently.'

'Yes, let's just hope it continues,' he replied.

Clementine wondered whether she should run upstairs and see if her great-aunt was all right.

Lady Clarissa placed a glass of milk and the half chocolate eclair on the table in front of her daughter. 'Oh, look! Lavender, you're such a

funny little thing,' she said, turning her head towards the fireplace.

Clemmie glanced around. She couldn't see anything unusual. Lavender was just sitting in her basket with Pharaoh beside her. As she turned back to her plate, she noticed a large bite missing from her eclair. Her mother was licking her fingers and hurrying back to the stove.

'Mummy!' the girl shouted. 'You ate my eclair.'

Her mother chortled. 'Sorry, Clemmie, I couldn't help myself. It just looked too good. Besides, you don't want to spoil your dinner, do you?'

Clementine giggled. Uncle Digby was laughing too. Now, Clementine thought, if only she could get Aunt Violet to laugh more, things would be just about perfect.

'I can't wait for tomorrow,' Clementine said as she gobbled the last bite of her afternoon tea.

'I was talking with Poppy's mother this afternoon and she's very excited too. She's planning a sausage sizzle for your lunch,' said Lady Clarissa.

The telephone rang and Clementine slid off her chair and ran to pick it up.

'Good afternoon, Penberthy House, this is Clementine. How may I help you?' she said confidently. Her mother and Uncle Digby turned around and smiled at Clemmie. She was becoming very good at answering the phone and Uncle Digby said that they might have to start paying her pocket money for being the hotel receptionist.

'I'll just get Mummy,' she said, and put her hand over the mouthpiece.

'Who is it, darling?' Lady Clarissa brushed her hands against her apron and walked towards Clementine.

Clemmie shrugged. 'They didn't say.'

Lady Clarissa frowned as she took the phone. 'Good afternoon, this is Clarissa Appleby.'

Clementine and Uncle Digby couldn't help hearing Lady Clarissa's responses.

'Oh, a recommendation from Mrs Fox?

That's wonderful. Yes, it was a beautiful wedding . . . Tomorrow? I'm afraid I can't tomorrow . . . I see. I'll have to think what I can do . . . I'll just write that number down and I'll get back to you in a little while.' And with that Clarissa hung up the phone.

'That sounded interesting.' Digby was now stirring apples on the stovetop. The sugar and cloves mixed in with the simmering fruit filled the kitchen with sweet smells.

'Yes, it seems Mrs Fox has been telling people about how wonderful Harriet's wedding was. That was a lady called Mrs Wilde. She wants to come and have a look at the house for her own daughter's wedding later in the year.'

'Another wedding?' Clementine gasped. She had so enjoyed the first one and couldn't wait for there to be another.

'Yes, but I'm afraid we might not be able to do it. Her daughter has just flown in from overseas and will be here for a couple of days. They can only come tomorrow and they can't be sure what time they'll get here.'

Clementine's face fell. 'But my excursion's tomorrow.'

'I can meet with them,' Uncle Digby said.

Lady Clarissa shook her head. 'You have your appointment with the doctor and you're not missing it.'

Digby frowned. 'Oh no, I'm afraid not.'

'What about Aunt Violet?' Clementine asked hopefully. 'Couldn't she show the people around?'

Lady Clarissa and Uncle Digby looked at one another. 'I don't think that's a good idea. Aunt Violet isn't exactly our best advertisement,' her mother said.

Clementine sighed. It was true. The last time Aunt Violet had been left in charge of the guests was on the weekend of the wedding. She'd rearranged the bedroom allocations and had an awful argument with Mrs Fox.

Digby frowned. 'Surely there's some way we can manage it. That repair quote for the roof was much more than we'd expected, Clarissa. Another wedding would just about cover it.'

Clarissa nodded. For years she'd put off the huge job of re-doing the roof, and dotted buckets around the house to catch the drips each time it rained. The builder had recently discovered a rather more sinister patch of damp in one of the upstairs bedrooms and said that if she didn't have the roof repaired soon, it could collapse completely.

Clementine was thinking. She knew that getting the roof fixed was important and Uncle Digby couldn't miss his doctor's appointment.

'Do you think Aunt Violet would like to come on the excursion?' she asked.

'Well, I don't know. Would you really be happy to take Aunt Violet with you?' her mother asked.

Clementine nodded. 'It might make her feel better.'

'What do you mean, sweetheart?'

'It might cheer her up,' Clementine replied.

Clarissa still wasn't following. She didn't know if something specific had upset Aunt Violet or she was in one of her usual grumps.

'I think it's more a question of would Aunt Violet want to go?' Uncle Digby added.

'I'll ask her.' Clementine jumped off her chair and walked over to the basket near the fireplace. She reached in to pick Pharaoh up.

'What are you doing with puss?' her mother asked.

'Aunt Violet always says that Pharaoh doesn't spend much time with her any more, so I thought I'd take him upstairs so he can have a visit.'

Digby winked at Clemmie. 'Good idea.'

Clementine cradled the bald cat in her arms and walked up the back stairs towards Aunt Violet's bedroom.

'Well, that's a turn up for the books,' said Digby.

'I just hope Aunt Violet says yes,' Lady Clarissa replied.

A QUESTION

Clementine shifted Pharaoh onto one arm and knocked gently on the door of the Blue Room.

There was no answer.

'Aunt Violet,' she called. 'May I come in?'

Violet Appleby was sitting at her dressing table, arranging the roses she'd cut earlier in a pretty crystal vase.

Clementine knocked again, a little louder. She was having trouble balancing Pharaoh and knocking at the same time, and hoped Aunt Violet would hurry up and answer.

Aunt Violet caught her finger on a rogue thorn and cursed as a tiny spot of blood oozed from her skin.

'What is it now?' the old woman called.

Clementine turned the handle and entered the room.

'Phew, I thought I was going to drop him. Pharaoh wanted to say hello.' She walked across the room and deposited the cat onto her great-aunt's lap.

'Well, it's about time you paid me a visit, my boy.' Aunt Violet nuzzled her face against Pharaoh's and he began to purr.

Clementine loved his motor. It was loud, like a sports car engine. She sometimes wished Lavender could purr, but she could grunt and squeak and that was cute too.

Clementine studied the crystal bowl of roses. 'Is that Granny's vase?'

'What if it is?' Aunt Violet asked.

'It's not allowed out of the sitting room cabinet,' Clementine explained. 'Mummy says it's too valuable.'

'Well, it looks lovely right where it is and I'll thank you not to blab to your mother or Pertwhistle. I'll put it back when I'm finished with it,' said Aunt Violet tartly.

Clementine frowned. She usually told her mother and Uncle Digby everything. She didn't like the idea of keeping a secret from them.

Aunt Violet looked at Clementine. 'Is that all?'

Clemmie shook her head. 'I was wondering . . .'

There was a short silence.

'Yes, yes, what is it?' Her great-aunt sighed impatiently. 'I haven't got all day, you know. Some of us have things to do.'

Clementine wondered exactly what it was that Aunt Violet had to do. She never seemed especially busy. Not like her mother and Uncle Digby.

'Well, you know how my class is going to Poppy's farm tomorrow and Mummy is supposed to come?' Clementine said.

Aunt Violet nodded. 'Yes. So?'

'Mummy can't come any more. Someone

wants to look at the house for a wedding and she says that it's best if she's here, and Uncle Digby said you can't be trusted to talk to people after last time.'

'What? That's outrageous!' Aunt Violet snapped. 'I'll thank Pertwhistle to keep his opinions to himself.'

'But you had a fight with Mrs Fox, remember?' Clementine reminded the old woman.

Violet Appleby rolled her eyes. 'The woman was a tyrant. Why don't you take Pertwhistle? It would be good to have him out of the house. Old codger's always sneaking up on me. He gives me the willies.'

'Uncle Digby can't come because he has to go to the doctor,' Clementine said. 'So I was wondering if you would come instead.'

'Me? Go to a farm? With all those smelly children?' She wrinkled her nose. 'No. It's out of the question. I have too many things to do. Do you think I sit around the house twiddling my thumbs all day?'

Clementine didn't realise that her aunt wasn't expecting an answer. She nodded.

'You do sit around the house. I don't know about twiddling your thumbs.'

The old woman pursed her lips. 'I do not! I'll have you know that I'm a very busy person.'

'Mummy says that if you give a busy person something extra to do, they'll always fit it in,' Clementine said.

'She would say that.' Violet Appleby paused for a moment. 'Why would you want me to come anyway?'

'Because I thought it might cheer you up and it will be fun,' Clementine replied.

'Fun?' her great-aunt repeated absently. She couldn't remember the last time she'd had fun. 'No, Clementine, I can't.'

Clementine's face fell. Aunt Violet was just about the most confusing person she'd ever met. They'd had some lovely times reading books together lately and Aunt Violet had even put Clementine to bed the other week, but now she was being so mean.

'Well, I don't want you to come anyway,' Clementine whispered.

'What did you say, Clementine?'

'I don't want you to come,' the child said, a little louder.

'So you ask me and then you don't really want me at all,' her great-aunt accused. 'Well, that's lovely, that is.'

'But you said that you didn't want to and you're too busy,' Clementine said.

'Well, now I think I might.' Aunt Violet stood up and deposited Pharaoh onto the four-poster bed.

'You might what?' Clementine asked cautiously.

'I might come along, if that's all right with you, Miss Change-Your-Mind,' said Aunt Violet.

'Really? You're not just saying that?' Clementine thought it was Aunt Violet who should be called Miss Change-Your-Mind.

Aunt Violet nodded. 'I said I would. But I'd better not have to look after any of those snotty brats.'

Clementine shook her head. 'Mrs Bottomley said that she only invited parents to come because she had to. She said they really wouldn't be much use.'

Violet Appleby raised her eyebrows. 'Did she now? We'll see about that.'

Clementine didn't know if she should feel happy that Aunt Violet had said yes, or worried that it could turn out like the pet day at school. On that day, Aunt Violet and Pharaoh had won the prize for pet most like its owner, even though Aunt Violet hadn't entered the competition. But at least now her mother would be able to meet the lady about the wedding and they could get the roof fixed.

Clementine walked to the door and then turned back to Aunt Violet. The woman was flicking through a magazine. 'Are you really sure?'

'Yes,' her great-aunt replied. 'But if you don't run along, I might just change my mind.'

Clementine nodded and scurried out of the room and down the main stairs.

She stopped on the landing and looked up at the portraits hanging on the wall. 'Hello

Granny and Grandpa. Aunt Violet is coming on the farm excursion. Can you believe it?'

Clementine could have sworn that her grandfather shook his head ever so slightly.

'I hope she's on her best behaviour,' Clementine said.

Uncle Digby was standing in the hallway below. He wondered how on earth Clementine had convinced her great-aunt to say yes.

Clementine addressed her granny's portrait. 'And I hope she doesn't upset any of the animals, or Mrs Bottomley.'

Digby grinned. Aunt Violet with twenty children and Mrs Bottomley at a farm – he rather hoped that the doctor might postpone his appointment after all, because he would have liked to see that for himself.

ROLL CALL

Clementine glanced up from where she was eating her cereal at the kitchen table. 'You look nice, Aunt Violet.' Her great-aunt was wearing a white pants-suit with a pair of shiny red ballet flats. She wore a large pearl choker around her neck. 'But don't you think you might get dirty?'

'I wasn't planning on it.' The old woman pulled out a chair and sat down.

'I think Clementine's right, Aunt Violet. White on a school excursion might be a little

46

risky,' Lady Clarissa said diplomatically. 'Especially to a farm.'

'I wear white all the time, Clarissa. I'll be fine.' Aunt Violet poured herself a cup of tea from the pot in the middle of the table.

'Until you have to feed something,' said Digby Pertwhistle. He was buttering several slices of toast.

'I won't be doing any of that,' Aunt Violet replied. 'I'm only going because Clarissa has pressing business and you have that silly doctor's appointment, which is a waste of time if you ask me. There doesn't seem to be anything wrong with you.'

'Thank you for your learned opinion, Dr Appleby,' Digby replied.

Clementine frowned. 'Are you a doctor, Aunt Violet?' This was the first she'd heard of such a thing. Her great-aunt certainly hadn't acted like a doctor when Uncle Digby had needed to go to hospital.

'No, Clementine, Uncle Digby is just teasing,' said her mother. She sat down and picked up the teapot. 'Of course he needs to go for his check-up. We wouldn't want anything to happen to him.'

'Well, that's a matter of opinion,' Aunt Violet murmured. 'Anyway, Clementine, you're not exactly in farm attire yourself.'

The children had been allowed to wear casual clothes for the day. 'This is an old dress,' Clementine replied. 'I love it but I won't be able to wear it much longer because I'm getting too big. I'm nearly five and a half now.'

'Well, it is . . . rather sweet,' her great-aunt replied.

Clementine was surprised to hear her say so.

Lady Clarissa glanced at the clock in the kitchen. 'Heavens, look at the time. Clemmie, run along and brush your teeth.'

Clementine pushed her chair out and hopped down. 'Look, our shoes match,' she said to Aunt Violet before scurrying away up the back stairs.

It wasn't long before Clementine farewelled

her mother and Uncle Digby and she and Aunt Violet were in the car heading towards Highton Mill. Clementine was glad that her great-aunt didn't seem to be in quite as much of a hurry as she was earlier in the week.

As they arrived in the street, there was an old red bus sitting outside the school gates.

'Where am I supposed to park?' Aunt Violet complained.

Clementine craned her neck to see if there were any spaces on the other side of the road. She pointed and said, 'I think there's a spot down there.'

Aunt Violet pressed her foot hard on the accelerator. There was another car heading towards them and she was determined to get to the parking space first.

'Ahh!' Clementine exclaimed and covered her eyes as Aunt Violet did a U-turn in front of the oncoming car. The old woman screeched to a halt in the space and smiled smugly.

Joshua Tribble's father rolled down the

passenger window and started shouting and gesturing wildly.

'That was my spot!' he yelled, then realised who he was speaking to. 'You again!'

Aunt Violet turned her head and looked the other way, pretending not to notice. 'I didn't see your name on it,' she said under her breath.

'I think Mr Tribble's upset,' Clementine said.

'He'll get over it.' Aunt Violet opened the driver's door and got out. Mr Tribble sped away.

Clementine hopped out onto the footpath. She slung her small pink backpack onto her shoulders and closed the door carefully.

Clementine bounced along beside her great-aunt until they reached the crossing in front of the school gates. She stopped and held out her hand.

Aunt Violet strode onto the road ahead of her.

'Aunt Violet,' Clementine called.

The old woman turned her head. 'What are you doing back there?'

'You have to hold my hand,' Clementine said. 'It's the rules.'

'Oh.' Aunt Violet walked back to the kerb. Clementine slipped her hand into Aunt Violet's.

Just inside the school gates, a crowd of children and a small group of parents milled about. Mrs Bottomley was there too, armed with a large clipboard and with a floppy straw hat on her head.

Aunt Violet narrowed her eyes. 'Good heavens, what is that woman wearing?'

It seemed that Mrs Bottomley had abandoned her usual brown checked suit in favour of a pair of brown corduroy trousers and a pasty-looking beige shirt. On her feet she wore dark green wellington boots. She'd been up before dawn going over the plans for the day and couldn't understand why her tummy was a little knotted. The thought occurred to her that she had always felt that way as a child, just before something exciting was about to happen. But surely that couldn't be the reason for her discomfort.

'Good morning, everyone,' the teacher called over the din. 'I need you to make two straight lines, in alphabetical order.'

Several of the children began to move. The parents, most of whom had come to wave the group off, continued chatting. Clementine looked up at Aunt Violet and pulled her towards the teacher.

Ethel Bottomley surveyed the chaotic scene in front of her and raised the whistle around her neck to her lips. The shrill squeal silenced everyone and she repeated her instruction.

'Children, two straight lines. NOW!' The whole class scampered into formation. They were so used to lining up in alphabetical order by now that it took no longer than half a minute. The parents didn't know what to do, so they stood at the back.

'We need to mark the roll,' Mrs Bottomley said. 'Clementine Appleby.'

'Yes, Mrs Bottomley,' Clemmie said.

'Angus Archibald,' Mrs Bottomley continued.

'Yes, Na–'

His grandmother shot him a nasty look.

'I mean, Mrs Bottomley,' Angus replied.

The teacher called each name until the whole class was checked off.

'I don't know why she couldn't have just counted you all,' Aunt Violet whispered to Clementine.

Clementine looked up. 'But she always calls the roll.'

'It wastes an awful lot of time, if you ask me,' Aunt Violet said.

Clementine could only agree. She'd thought that from her first day.

'Now the parents,' Mrs Bottomley began. 'If you're not joining us, please move away from the children.'

'Godfathers,' Aunt Violet muttered. 'Is the woman incapable of counting a handful of adults?'

'Lady Appleby?'

'It's Miss Appleby and yes,' Aunt Violet replied tersely.

Ethel Bottomley looked up from where she was ticking off the list of names.

'No, you're not coming. Clementine's mother is joining us.'

'There's been a change of plans,' Aunt Violet replied. 'My niece has been caught up at home and I will be coming instead.'

Mrs Bottomley's lips twitched. 'But I was expecting Lady Appleby.'

'Well, you'll just have to make do with Miss Appleby instead,' said Aunt Violet.

'You're not exactly dressed for it,' Mrs Bottomley scolded.

Aunt Violet looked the teacher up and down and sneered. 'I don't know, Mrs Bottomley. Someone needed to inject a little bit of style into this occasion. Clearly that wasn't on your agenda.'

Ethel Bottomley frowned. She decided to ignore the woman's last comment.

Sophie's mother, Odette, was there too, along with Joshua Tribble's father. Mrs Bauer and her husband would meet the group at the farm with Poppy, who'd been allowed to stay home that morning.

'All right, everyone, before we get on the bus I want to go over our list of rules,' Mrs

Bottomley barked. 'Who can tell me one of them?'

Hands shot into the air.

'Yes, Sophie?' The woman pointed at the dark-haired child.

'Don't wander off.'

'Good. Anyone else?'

'Don't touch the animals,' another voice called.

Mrs Bottomley nodded.

'Don't eat anything from the garden,' Astrid said.

'Yes, I don't want anyone getting sick,' Mrs Bottomley replied.

Violet Appleby raised her hand.

The teacher wondered what the old woman had to offer. She hesitated then pointed at her.

'Don't have any fun,' Aunt Violet said with a straight face. There was a titter of laughter from the other parents and some of the children.

'Of course we're going to have fun, Miss Appleby. Orderly fun,' Mrs Bottomley sneered.

'It doesn't sound like much fun to me,' Aunt Violet scoffed. 'Fancy going to a farm and telling the children they can't touch the animals. The only reason I agreed to Clementine's request to come along was that she told me there was fun in the offing. I'm not hearing that at the moment.'

Joshua's father leaned over to Sophie's mother and whispered, 'I never imagined Miss Appleby and I would agree on anything, but the woman's quite right.'

Odette Rousseau chuckled.

Clementine wished that Aunt Violet would stop talking. She could see Mrs Bottomley's ears turning pink and she looked crosser than usual.

'First and foremost, Miss Appleby, it is my duty to ensure that the children in my care are safe at all times. And that they learn something. Now if you're quite finished, you can board the bus.'

THE BUS RIDE

Clementine walked up the steps. A round man wearing a brown shirt and shorts, and long beige socks was sitting behind the steering wheel. He had curly brown hair too, and Clementine wondered if he was related to Mrs Bottomley.

'Good morning, miss,' the man said with a smile. 'My name's Bernie Stubbs.'

'Good morning,' Clementine smiled back.

'I think we're in for a good day,' he said and gave her a wink.

Clementine decided then that he couldn't be related to Mrs Bottomley. He was much too happy and friendly.

She walked into the aisle and wondered where to sit. Aunt Violet, who had entered the bus behind her, had already made up her mind.

'Clementine, here,' her great-aunt said as she slid into the front seat on the passenger side.

'But Mrs Bottomley said that we have to keep the front seats free for people who get bus sick,' Clementine protested.

'I don't care what Mrs Bottomley said. We're sitting here.' Aunt Violet pursed her lips and Clementine slipped in beside her. 'I'm not going any further into this contraption than is absolutely necessary.'

The other children streamed onto the vehicle and raced towards the back. By the time Mrs Bottomley walked up the steps everyone had found a seat – although Joshua and Angus were playing a rowdy game and rushing up and down the aisle.

'You boys stop that at once,' Mrs Bottomley shouted, then blew her whistle. Joshua and Angus sat behind Mr Tribble, who had been trying unsuccessfully to get the two boys to settle down.

Mrs Bottomley gave him a stern look and then glanced at Aunt Violet. She was about to say something but Aunt Violet got in first.

'Clementine mentioned that the front seats were reserved for people who weren't good travellers,' the old woman said. 'And we wouldn't want anyone in the back of the bus to suffer if someone's feeling a bit peaky.' Aunt Violet motioned at Clementine, and Mrs Bottomley kept her mouth closed. She could have sworn that there was nothing on the child's medical form about travel sickness but she didn't feel like having another argument with Miss Appleby.

The driver, who had hopped off the bus to make some last-minute checks, reappeared and lumbered back to his seat.

'Good morning, Ethel. You're looking lovely today,' he said, grinning at Mrs Bottomley.

A crimson flush rose on Mrs Bottomley's cheeks and she giggled like a schoolgirl. No one had told her that in years.

The bus driver turned the key in the ignition and the vehicle sputtered.

'All aboard?' he asked, glancing at Mrs Bottomley.

'Wait a minute. I have to call the roll.'

'Again?' Aunt Violet said. 'Surely you could just count everyone.'

Ethel Bottomley held onto her clipboard like a drowning sailor to a lifebuoy. She pulled out her pen.

'Would you like this?' Mr Stubbs offered her a small microphone.

Mrs Bottomley took it from him and pushed the button on the side of the handpiece. It crackled to life.

'When everyone is in their seats I will do a final check of the roll before we head off.'

There was an audible groan from Aunt Violet, and Mrs Bottomley noticed that Mr Tribble rolled his eyes too.

She ignored them both and ran down the list, checking off the names.

'All present and accounted for,' said Mrs Bottomley, tapping her pen on the page.

The bus lurched forward and Mrs Bottomley wobbled on her feet.

'Heavens, Mr Stubbs, you could have waited a moment.' Mrs Bottomley clutched the pole beside the driver and swung into her seat behind him. 'I almost ended up in your lap.'

'That wouldn't have been so bad now, Ethel, would it?' he chuckled.

'I think you should keep your eyes on the road, driver,' Aunt Violet said loudly.

Ethel Bottomley's face was redder than a beetroot. She ignored Miss Appleby's comment and set to arranging her handbag beside her.

Clementine looked out of the window as the bus passed by the little row of shops where Sophie's father had his patisserie. Her tummy fluttered. She turned to her great-aunt and declared, 'Today is going to be fun!'

Her great-aunt nodded. 'If you say so.'

Clementine reached out and put her hand into Aunt Violet's. To her surprise, the old woman gave it a squeeze.

The bus bumped along to the other side of the village. The farm at Highton Hall wasn't too far away but required the driver to navigate some narrow country lanes.

'Perhaps we should have a song,' Sophie's mother suggested loudly. She started a rousing chorus of 'The Wheels on the Bus'.

Mrs Bottomley leaned forward and gestured at the microphone. 'Give me that, Mr Stubbs.'

He grinned in the rear-vision mirror. 'Oh good, are we going to have some karaoke?'

'Certainly not,' said the teacher. 'Children, please stop that singing at once. You're distracting Mr Stubbs.'

'Oh no, I love a good singalong,' the driver protested.

'You're not being very helpful, Mr Stubbs,' Mrs Bottomley whispered.

'I just thought it would be nice to have a song,' the man replied.

'Goodness no,' Ethel Bottomley said quietly, then looked over at Clementine. 'Children, all this noise is, um, upsetting Clementine. We don't want to make her sick, do we?'

'But I don't get bus–' Clementine began to protest then felt a nudge from her great-aunt.

Aunt Violet gave Clemmie a freezing stare. The singing stopped. For a few minutes all that could be heard was the drone of the engine as Mr Stubbs wrestled the old beast down a gear and headed up the hill.

Soon the bus slowed and Mr Stubbs turned off the road and through a grand set of gates. They were now on the estate of Highton Hall.

The main house was quite a distance away, through another set of gates on the left. But the bus continued right, down a tree-lined drive dappled with sunlight. They passed several cottages and at the end of the road, the bus pulled up outside a hotchpotch of sheds.

'Look, there's Poppy!' Clementine exclaimed as her friend came running towards them.

The atmosphere on the bus had risen to fever pitch with everyone jostling to see what was going on outside.

'There's a duck,' one of the boys called.

'I can see a cow over there,' another child shouted.

'Children, get back into your seats and sit down,' Mrs Bottomley yelled. She snatched the microphone before Mr Stubbs had time to pass it to her.

She instructed the children to stay where they were and then hopped off the bus to find Mr Bauer, who would be taking the group on a tour of the farm. She was eager to go over the schedule with him one last time. Poppy said hello and Heinrich Bauer appeared from around the side of one of the sheds.

'Good morning, Mrs Bottomley,' he said in his thick German accent. 'It is good to see you.'

'Yes,' said Mrs Bottomley. 'I suppose I should thank you for inviting us.'

'I see the children are excited.' Mr Bauer

nodded towards the bus, which had lots of little faces pressed up against the windows.

'A little too excited for my liking,' Mrs Bottomley replied. 'You'll need to take a firm hand with them, Mr Bauer. I certainly will. If anyone gets up to mischief they'll be locked up in the dairy.'

'Don't worry, Mrs Bottomley. The children will be fine. I have lots of things for them to see and they will be too tired to get up to any mischief-making.'

Mrs Bottomley reached for her schedule but the man had already jumped onto the bus and begun to welcome the children loudly.

'My name is Heinrich Bauer and you know my little girl, Poppy,' he said. 'Now we are going to have a lovely time on the farm today but you must make sure that you follow my instructions. Most of all, I want everyone to have some fun today.'

Aunt Violet was glad to hear it. At least Mr Bauer seemed excited to have the children visiting.

GRANNY BERT

A little way back down the lane was Rose Cottage. It was home to Albertine Rumble, known to almost everyone in the district as Granny Bert. As the old red bus clunked by, the woman woke from a nap and remembered that Lily Bauer had invited her to morning tea. Her granddaughter Daisy had already left for work at the doctor's surgery. The girl assisted Dr Everingham in Highton Mill three days a week and helped out at Highton Hall two other days.

Daisy had helped choose her grandmother's clothes that morning and left her with some sandwiches for her lunch. She hated leaving the old woman on her own, as Granny seemed to be getting more and more forgetful by the day. But at least Lily and Heinrich were close by and Mrs Greening, who lived with her husband in the Gatehouse, often dropped in to check on her too.

Granny Bert pulled on her cardigan and gathered up her handbag and walking stick. She never went anywhere without either one. She wobbled her way downstairs and out through the back door, taking the path to the front of the cottage. She was surprised to see a bus parked beside the hay shed and wondered where it had come from. Granny walked towards it and saw that the door was open. She poked her head inside and drew in a deep breath. There was something about the smell that brought back all sorts of memories.

She used to ride on the bus all the time. She'd go into the village, and sometimes much further, to see her sister who lived in Downsfordvale. Granny Bert smiled to herself, remembering the lovely feeling of the bus swaying and the excitement of a new adventure.

Lily Bauer had been rushing about all morning. She was just about to take the brownies out of the oven when Poppy called out that the bus had arrived. At least she had a few minutes to spare while Heinrich organised the children. He said that he'd take them straight to the henhouse to collect the eggs, which she planned to boil up and have as part of their lunch.

Her brownies looked perfect and smelt delicious. She popped them on the sink to cool and checked on the scones she'd baked earlier, scurrying about to fill the jam and cream pots.

Having awoken to a sky as big and blue as the sea, she'd asked Heinrich to set up a row of trestle tables outside, which she planned to use at morning tea and lunch. They'd had the hay shed on standby in case of bad weather but it looked as if they'd be able to enjoy the outdoors. There were enough chairs for the adults but the children would have to sit on the grass. Lily didn't think they'd mind.

She wondered if she'd have time to pop over and get Granny Bert. The woman had never fully recovered from a bout of illness earlier in the year and she certainly wasn't the same robust old lady they knew and loved.

Lily glanced at the clock and decided that Granny would have to make her own way over from Rose Cottage if she remembered, or no one would be getting fed at all.

SCRAMBLED EGGS

Heinrich Bauer led his visitors through the gate and around the back of the pretty stone cottage the Bauers called home. Clementine stood beside Sophie and Poppy. The three girls giggled with excitement.

Suddenly, Poppy whispered, 'What's your Aunt Violet doing here?' She had just noticed the old woman chatting to the other parents.

'I asked her,' said Clementine.

Poppy frowned. 'Why?'

'Mummy had an important meeting and Uncle Digby had to go to the doctor and I thought she might like to come.'

'Is she going to be nice?' Poppy asked.

'I hope so. But you can never tell with Aunt Violet. She's unper . . . un-pre-dictable. But she was good on the bus.'

Mr Bauer told the children about some of the plans for the morning. 'We will be having a look at the chickens and the pigs and I think we might even find someone to help milk the cow.'

'Cool!' Joshua said. 'That'll be me.'

Mrs Bottomley was standing right behind the boy. 'We'll see about that,' she replied.

'If you will follow me, we will see if the chickens have been busy this morning,' said Heinrich.

'Two straight lines,' Mrs Bottomley called as she watched the children amble off. She blew loudly on her whistle. 'Where are your partners?'

'The woman will give herself an aneurysm,' Aunt Violet whispered. Joshua Tribble's father was standing right beside her, and chortled to himself.

Aunt Violet turned and stared.

'I didn't think I'd like you at all, you old parking-spot thief! But you're actually quite funny,' he said.

Aunt Violet rolled her eyes. 'You haven't heard the half of it.'

Lily Bauer came out of the kitchen and said hello. She advised Mrs Bottomley that there were tea and scones for the adults in the garden.

The teacher shook her head sharply. 'We must go with the children.'

'You told the children the parents wouldn't be any use on the excursion anyway,' said Aunt Violet archly. 'So I'm happy to accept your invitation, Mrs Bauer. A cup of tea is just what's needed.'

'I did no such thing,' insisted Mrs Bottomley. She was trying to remember if she'd actually said that out loud at any point. She knew she'd thought it.

At the far end of the garden, Mr Bauer was leading the children towards a high stone wall. The henhouse was on the other side. He opened a timber door set into the stone and called, 'Come on, everyone.' Mrs Bottomley was trotting behind them, doing her best to catch up.

'Wow, it's like a hotel for hens,' one of the little boys exclaimed.

'Thank you, young man,' Heinrich said, grinning. 'We are very proud of our chickens. They give us eggs for the whole estate.'

Mrs Bottomley was horrified to see that Mr Bauer had taken all of the children inside the henhouse. She stood back from the doorway and crowed, 'Mr Bauer, do you think it's a good idea to have those children in there with all of those feathers and claws?'

'Of course, Mrs Bottomley,' the man called back. 'Please come inside and shut the door.'

Rows of hens – white, black, grey and red – sat in their boxes, clucking away.

Heinrich pointed at a pretty black speckled

hen, which was making a very loud noise. 'Can anyone tell me what she is doing in there?'

'She's tired,' Angus said.

Heinrich shook his head. 'No, I don't think so.'

'She's lazy,' Joshua called.

'B-cark, b-cark, b-cark.' The hen's clucking was getting louder and higher with each call.

Clementine put up her hand and waited to be asked.

Heinrich pointed to her. 'Yes, Clementine.'

'I think she's just laid an egg,' Clementine replied.

Heinrich walked up to the box and reached in underneath the fowl. He pulled out a light-brown egg.

Everyone cheered.

'Would you like to hold it, Clementine?' Mr Bauer asked. She nodded and held out her hands. Heinrich placed the egg down gently.

'It's warm,' Clementine said with a grin.

'I need some helpers to collect the eggs today,' the man said. He picked up three wicker baskets.

Everyone wanted to have a turn, so Heinrich asked Mrs Bottomley to choose six children who could go to different parts of the henhouse.

'Astrid. You can choose someone to take with you,' Mrs Bottomley said. Astrid selected Sophie.

Next, the teacher called to the tallest lad in the class, who seemed to wear a permanent frown. 'Lester, you can choose someone as well.' The boy pointed at Eddie Whipple.

'And Angus, why don't you ask someone to help you too,' Mrs Bottomley finished.

Joshua was ready to jump as soon as Angus said his name. But this time, Angus didn't.

'Angus, who would you like to be your helper?' Mrs Bottomley asked again.

The curly-haired boy pointed.

'Clementine,' Angus said.

Joshua snorted loudly.

Clementine was surprised to hear her name. She wondered if he'd meant to say it.

Joshua kicked at the dirt. 'That's his girl-friend.'

'Is not.' Angus shot Joshua a sneer.

No one else said a word.

Heinrich handed out the baskets and nodded at Mrs Bottomley. While the teacher watched the six children make their way through the henhouse, he took the rest of the class out through another door to show them where the geese slept each evening. Apparently they were roaming around the bottom field, nowhere near the henhouse. This was just as well, as Mrs Bottomley felt very uneasy about the geese. The creatures had a bad reputation for behaving like guard dogs, and she wasn't keen for her students to disturb them.

Inside with the chickens, Angus had found three eggs already and Clementine spotted another two. Clementine made sure that she deposited each new egg slowly, so it didn't clunk against the others. Angus did the same. They continued checking each box.

At the other end of the building, Astrid and Sophie were excitedly counting their eggs

and Eddie and Lester were going about their business very seriously too.

Heinrich reappeared and beckoned the children to come out and show the rest of the class their treasures.

Astrid and Sophie had eight eggs, Eddie and Lester had collected nine and Angus and Clementine had found a record-breaking thirteen.

The class was very impressed with the haul.

'I know that seems like a lot,' Heinrich explained. 'But many people live on the estate. Lily makes up cartons and delivers them to Mrs Oliver up at the Hall, Mrs Greening and Granny Bert, and if there are too many we give them to the neighbours as well. We seem to get through them and it's bad news if the girls stop laying. Last year they went on strike for a month and there were no eggs for anyone.'

'Why did they do that?' Astrid asked. 'Did they want a better henhouse?'

Heinrich Bauer smiled. 'No, they already

have the best henhouse. I discovered Mr Fox was paying them a visit each night. He couldn't get in but he spent a long time staring at the girls. I think it made them very nervous.'

'Did you shoot him?' Joshua asked. 'Because I would shoot him.'

Sophie frowned at him. 'What with? Your water pistol?'

Heinrich Bauer shook his head. 'Mr Fox has been relocated.'

Clementine wondered what that meant.

'Children, would you carry the eggs up to the house and leave them at the back door for Lily?' Heinrich directed.

Mrs Bottomley could sniff an impending disaster. 'Do you really think that's a good idea, Mr Bauer?'

'It will be fine,' the man replied.

The egg collectors walked in pairs on either side of their baskets, carrying their treasures carefully. Clementine and Angus were the last to go, and just as Clementine was walking past Joshua, the boy stretched out his foot.

'Ahhhh!' Clementine cried out as she thudded to the ground. The eggs spilled everywhere, splattering all over the lawn and on Angus's t-shirt as well.

'Why did you do that?' Angus yelled at Clementine and scrambled to his feet.

'I didn't.' Clemmie began to cry.

'What in heaven's name?' Mrs Bottomley swooped on the pair. 'What a mess! What a disaster! I knew the children couldn't be trusted with the eggs.'

Angus turned on Clementine. 'It was her fault. She tripped over and then she made me fall over too.'

Joshua had rushed ahead as soon as the pair had fallen and was now watching the drama and chuckling behind his hands.

'It was Joshua,' Clementine wailed. 'He tripped me.'

'Never mind,' Heinrich said. 'It was an accident.' He looked at Clementine's big blue eyes.

'I . . . I . . . I'm sorry,' she sobbed. 'I didn't mean to.'

'Of course you didn't mean to.' Heinrich patted the girl on the shoulder.

'I saw him,' Sophie told Clementine. 'Joshua tripped you over on purpose.'

'I did not,' Joshua lied. 'I wasn't even near her.'

Poppy stared at the boy, whose tongue shot out at her like the sneaky snake that he was.

'Angus doesn't believe me,' Clementine said.

'Don't worry about him,' said Sophie.

The children walked up to the back of the house where Lily had organised some fruit and brownies for their morning tea.

Lily took one look at Clementine and exclaimed, 'Oh dear, what's happened, Clemmie?' The little girl began to cry again.

'I smashed the eggs,' Clemmie sobbed.

'But it was an accident, I'm sure,' Lily said as she hugged Clementine.

'Look what she did to me,' Angus exclaimed. Raw egg dripped from his t-shirt.

'Never mind.' Odette Rousseau came to the

boy's rescue. 'I'm sure we can get that off. I'll get some wipes.'

Joshua Tribble was enjoying the scene in front of him. If Angus was going to choose a girl instead of him, then he'd have to pay for his decisions. His father noticed his smug smile and stalked across the yard, eager to find out if his son had been involved. Fortunately, the man wasn't easily fooled.

Aunt Violet approached Lily and Clementine.

'I remember breaking eggs once when I was your age. And I can tell you that your great-grandmother was much more concerned about it than Mr and Mrs Bauer. It might have had something to do with the timing, as Mama was hosting a dinner party for the Highton-Smiths that very evening and wanted her cook to show off all manner of tasty treats. I was sent to bed without any dinner.'

Clementine looked at her great-aunt and sniffled. 'Really?'

'I certainly was,' the old woman said. She

pulled a handkerchief from her pocket and dabbed at Clemmie's face.

'That sounds an entirely suitable punishment for today's behaviour,' Mrs Bottomley chimed in. 'Clementine, I think you can forget about having any of those brownies Mrs Bauer has made. You need to be more careful and less wasteful.'

'How dare you.' Aunt Violet drew herself up and stood over the stout teacher. 'It was an accident. Clementine is clearly sorry about what happened and she will eat exactly what the other children are eating.'

Mrs Bottomley was about to argue when she saw Joshua Tribble laughing loudly and pointing at Clementine.

'We'll discuss it later,' the old woman huffed, and bustled away.

'No, we won't!' Aunt Violet barked after her.

PIGS AND COWS

Clementine nibbled her chocolate brownie, wondering if Mrs Bottomley was going to appear at any moment and take it from her. Aunt Violet was keeping an eye on the situation too, determined that the woman would do no such thing.

Fortunately, the teacher was caught up sorting out a disagreement between some other children.

After morning tea, Mrs Bottomley insisted that everyone go to the toilet, including the parents. There would be no accidents on her watch. Unfortunately, the queue was rather long and the group was running far behind Mrs Bottomley's schedule.

'Two straight lines, children. Now!' the woman snapped before blowing her whistle.

'Godfathers!' Aunt Violet muttered. 'Does she really need to do that?'

Clementine rushed to her place at the head of the line, beside Angus. Despite Mrs Rousseau's best efforts with a wet wipe, his shirt was still splattered with egg yolk and starting to smell nasty too.

'I'm sorry about before,' Clementine whispered.

Angus shrugged. He didn't want to talk about it.

'Will the parents be joining us this time?' Mrs Bottomley called. It wasn't really a question.

Aunt Violet had been quite happy sitting in the sun, but as the other adults moved off she thought she'd better go too.

Lily Bauer looked around and realised that

Granny Bert had never arrived. 'Heinrich, I'm just going to see Granny Bert.'

'Oh, good idea, we forgot about her,' the man replied.

'I suspect she might have forgotten about us too,' Lily said hopefully.

'What are we doing now?' Sophie asked Heinrich.

'We will go to see the pigs,' he replied.

Sophie smiled.

The class followed Heinrich Bauer in two straight lines to the pigpen that was attached to the end of the barn. His wife walked with them then shot off down the lane to Rose Cottage to find Granny Bert.

The pigpen had a shelter in the corner, and water and feed troughs near the fence. A huge mother pig lay on some scattered straw with six piglets attached to her teats and suckling noisily. Over by the fence was a large mud puddle. Judging by the crusty patchwork of brown on the sow's body, she had enjoyed rolling in it.

Joshua held his nose. 'Pooh! They stink!'

'Does anyone know what pigs eat?' Heinrich asked, ignoring the lad's antics.

'Girls,' Joshua said.

Mrs Bottomley glared at the boy. Joshua's father poked him in the back and shook his head.

Heinrich pointed at Astrid, whose hand had been the first to go up.

'Pigs are omnivorous, which means they can eat vegetables and meat. Mostly people feed them vegetable scraps from the kitchen,' Astrid said. 'But the piglets are drinking milk from their mother.'

Heinrich nodded. 'You're a clever girl. We also give our pigs some kibble that we feed the dogs.'

'And sometimes they eat cupcakes,' Clementine announced.

'How ridiculous, Clementine.' Mrs Bottomley rolled her eyes. 'Pigs do not eat cupcakes.'

'Lavender does. She loves them, but we only let her have one on special occasions, like when it's someone's birthday.'

'Your pig is hardly the same as a farm pig, is she?' Mrs Bottomley said.

'Our pigs have been known to get the odd cake every now and then,' Heinrich confirmed. He grinned and continued, 'Mostly when Mrs Greening has been experimenting with her baking and things haven't turned out so well.'

Clementine smiled at Mr Bauer, who winked at her. Mrs Bottomley didn't know anything about pigs, Clemmie thought with satisfaction.

'Why are they so dirty?' one of the children called out.

'Pigs like to bathe in the mud because they don't sweat the way people do. It's a way for them to cool down. And it looks like fun too, don't you think?' Heinrich explained.

Some of the children nodded.

'Who'd like to hold one of the piglets?' Heinrich asked.

'I don't think that's a good idea, Mr Bauer,' Mrs Bottomley replied.

'It's all right, Mrs Bottomley. Good old Marta

would probably appreciate a rest for a few minutes.'

'No,' Mrs Bottomley protested. 'The children will get dirty.'

'But I love mud,' Joshua called.

A chorus of 'Me too!' went up.

Before she could say another word, Mr Bauer entered the pigpen and snatched up one of the wriggling piglets. It squeaked and oinked and the children laughed at all the noises it made.

The mother pig, Marta, raised her head, stared briefly at Mr Bauer, then laid it down again. The poor sow looked exhausted.

'Come along, Mrs Bottomley, would you like to hold her first?'

'No, no, get her away from me.' Ethel Bottomley waved her hands and ran in a circle with Mr Bauer and the piglet chasing after her.

'Come now, the teacher must set the good example for the students. She won't hurt you.'

The children roared with laughter. Mrs Bottomley turned around and Heinrich thrust the piglet into her arms.

'What do I do with her?' The woman grimaced and held tight to the squealing beast.

'Give her a cuddle, Mrs Bottomley,' Heinrich laughed.

'I'm not cuddling a pig,' the woman squawked.

'Oh, for goodness sake, give it to me.' Aunt Violet strode forward and snatched the creature from the teacher's hands.

Clementine's mouth gaped open.

Aunt Violet then passed the piglet to Clementine, who cradled the small pink beast in her arms.

'Settle down, little piggy,' Clemmie cooed. She tickled the creature under the chin. Much to everyone's surprise, it stopped wriggling and looked up at the girl.

'You have the magic touch, Clementine,' announced Heinrich. 'She knows you like pigs.'

Mrs Bottomley shot Aunt Violet a dirty look.

The children took turns holding the piglets.

'Thank you, Aunt Violet,' Clementine whispered to the old woman. Aunt Violet was

standing at the back of the group and watching the children as they delighted in holding the wriggling creatures.

'Think nothing of it, Clementine,' Aunt Violet replied. 'Your teacher was being ridiculous.'

Mrs Bottomley glared at Aunt Violet then glanced at her watch. 'Mr Bauer, we need to be getting a move on, don't you think?'

Heinrich nodded. 'Okay, children, piggies back to their mother. We are going to meet Constance now.'

'Who's Constance?' Joshua asked.

'Constance the cow,' Poppy replied.

Mrs Bottomley led the way into the yard. She blew on her whistle and the children hurried into formation.

'Surely the children can walk from one shed to another without the military parade,' Aunt Violet muttered. She didn't realise that Mrs Bottomley, like most teachers, had powerful hearing.

'I'd prefer we didn't lose anyone, Miss

Appleby,' Mrs Bottomley replied. 'If that's all right with you.'

Aunt Violet sighed and rolled her eyes.

The group marched towards the cowshed, where they found Constance. She was a beautiful tan-coloured jersey cow, and Clementine thought she had the longest eyelashes she'd ever seen.

'She's so pretty,' Sophie said.

Clementine nodded.

'Yes, doesn't know how lucky she is with those lashes,' Aunt Violet added.

The children stood on the railings surrounding the pen while Heinrich organised himself with a tiny three-legged stool and a stainless steel bucket.

'Who would like to help me milk Constance?' he asked.

Hands shot into the air from every direction.

The man grinned at the children. 'I don't think we'll ask Mrs Bottomley this time.'

'Yes, well, I'll thank you not to,' the old woman said through pursed lips.

'What about you, Miss Appleby? Would you like to go first and show the children how it's done?'

Aunt Violet frowned. She was about to say 'no' when the word 'yes' escaped from her lips.

Clementine looked at her great-aunt in amazement. 'Are you sure?'

'Well, I don't know, Clementine, but it doesn't look too difficult.'

Aunt Violet walked through the gate into the pen. She stroked Connie's forehead and looked into the old girl's eyes.

'Hello gorgeous,' she whispered, then ran her hand along the cow's bulging body.

'I think, Miss Appleby, you have done this before?' Heinrich said.

'A long time ago, Mr Bauer.' She crouched on the stool and positioned the shiny silver bucket under Connie's udder. She placed her hand on one of the beast's teats and pulled gently. A white stream pinged against the bottom of the bucket.

The children were mesmerised as they watched. The old woman was using both hands now and the bucket was filling fast.

'Miss Appleby, you are an expert,' Heinrich told Aunt Violet, who looked up with a sheepish grin.

'Not an expert, Mr Bauer, but not bad for an old lady,' she replied.

Clementine couldn't believe it. Aunt Violet was full of surprises today.

'Who'd like to go next?' the farmer asked.

There was no shortage of volunteers. Mr Bauer picked Ella, who was happy to receive some instruction from Aunt Violet. The woman seemed very pleased to be able to help each child as they came to have their turn.

Last of all Joshua slid onto the stool.

Aunt Violet had retreated to the other end of the shed to wash her hands, so Mr Bauer tried to instruct Joshua on his milking technique. The boy pulled down hard on one of Connie's teats with no luck. He pulled again.

Mrs Bottomley was hovering close by, as the

boy had been making a particular nuisance of himself. He'd been poking and pinching the other children and his father had very little control over him. He was lucky to be getting a turn at all.

'It's not fair, she's run out of milk,' Joshua complained.

He pulled again and tilted the teat upwards. This time a long stream of milk shot out, straight at Mrs Bottomley. It hit her right in the face.

Joshua laughed loudly.

'Joshua Tribble,' the woman bellowed as she wiped the milk from her cheek. 'Stop that at once.'

The boy was tempted to have another go. He looked around and saw his father glaring.

'Don't you even think about it, young man,' Mr Tribble growled.

Connie had stood patiently chewing on her cud for almost twenty minutes. But Mr Bauer noticed that her tail had begun to twitch.

'Mrs Bottomley, you should come away from there,' the man said.

'What is it now?'

The old woman turned just in time to see Connie lift her tail and deposit a stream of runny poo on the straw behind her.

'Arrrrgh!' Mrs Bottomley shrieked and jumped clear just as the mound began to build.

'Pooh! She stinks,' Joshua called out.

'Joshua Tribble, I do not stink,' Mrs Bottomley barked.

'I meant the cow,' he said. 'But your boots stink too.' The lad pointed at the teacher's wellington boots, which were now splattered brown as well.

Mrs Bottomley shook her head and stalked to the other end of the barn to look for a tap.

Heinrich Bauer took over and finished the last few minutes of milking, then carried the pail to the gate.

'What's next?' Clementine asked excitedly. She was having a wonderful day, despite the egg incident.

Lily Bauer came racing towards the group. 'Heinrich! I can't find Granny anywhere,' she puffed. 'I've been through Rose Cottage from top to bottom; I've scoured the sheds and called Daisy, and she said that Granny should be here.'

'Did you telephone the Hall and see if she's gone up there?' her husband asked.

'Yes, and I've spoken to Mrs Greening. No one has seen her at all,' Lily replied.

'I saw an old lady when we got here, near the bus,' said Joshua.

'What was she doing near the bus?' Heinrich asked.

'She was looking inside the door, when we were walking towards the house,' the boy replied.

'Oh dear, you don't think she could have hopped on and gone to the village with Mr Stubbs, do you?' Lily asked her husband.

'Who knows?' he said. 'But I don't have time to look for her now. I have to get the barbecue started for the sausage sizzle.'

'I'll call Mr Greening and see if he can head into town and look for her,' said Lily. 'Mrs

Greening said that she and Mrs Shillingsworth would go out on foot to look.'

'And we can help with the food,' Mr Tribble spoke up. Sophie's mother nodded too.

'Well, what am I supposed to do with the children?' Mrs Bottomley asked. She had returned to the group and was most unimpressed. Lost old ladies were not on her schedule.

'You could still go and see the lambs in the field,' Heinrich suggested.

Mrs Bottomley shook her head, aghast. 'We're not going on our own! It says here that someone called Mr Greening was going to take us to view the lambs.'

'Well, I'm afraid that we need him to go and search for Granny Bert. She's a frail old lady who hasn't been herself lately and we don't want anything to happen to her. I'm sure you can understand that,' Heinrich explained.

Ethel Bottomley just wanted a cup of tea and a lie down.

Aunt Violet intervened. 'We can find our way

to the field and back, Mrs Bottomley. It would be such a pity for the children to miss out on seeing the lambs.'

'No, we're staying here,' said Mrs Bottomley.

Aunt Violet looked at the children. 'Who wants to see the new lambs?' she asked.

'Me!' the children called in unison.

'I think you're outvoted, Mrs Bottomley.' Aunt Violet smiled at the woman and arched her eyebrow. 'Besides, Poppy lives on the farm. I'm sure we won't get lost with her in the lead.'

Poppy nodded like a jack-in-the-box. 'I know the farm backwards,' she confirmed.

'And me and Sophie have been here before,' Clementine added.

'Sophie and I, Clementine,' Mrs Bottomley corrected.

'That's settled, then. Let's go and find some lambs,' Aunt Violet commanded, as the children cheered.

LAMB TALES

The group set off with Poppy and Aunt Violet in the lead and Mrs Bottomley bringing up the rear. Joshua's father and Sophie's mother stayed behind to help with lunch and the search for Granny Bert.

The children would be having barbecued sausages in bread rolls baked fresh at Sophie's father's patisserie, salad from the garden, hard-boiled eggs from the chickens and milkshakes courtesy of Constance the cow for their lunch. Mrs Greening, who lived with her husband in the Gatehouse on the estate, had made one of her delicious cakes too. Nearly all of the food was from the farm.

Poppy led the class through a gate in the stone wall at the front of their cottage, and into the long meadow dotted with oak trees.

'Daddy said the lambs are over on the other side of the stream,' Poppy explained to Aunt Violet as they trotted along.

'Stream? Did I hear you say there was a stream, Poppy? We're not going near any water, are we?' Mrs Bottomley snapped.

Aunt Violet turned around. 'There's a bridge, you old fusspot,' she fumed at the teacher. She looked down at Poppy and whispered, 'There is a bridge, isn't there?'

The child nodded. 'Of course.'

Aunt Violet smiled, relieved.

Clementine and Sophie were walking a little further behind.

'What happened to her?' Sophie asked, pointing at Clemmie's great-aunt.

Clementine shrugged. 'I don't know. I think

Grandpa must have told her to be on her best behaviour today.'

'Do you think she'll turn back?' Sophie whispered.

'Into what?' Clementine asked.

'Herself,' Sophie said.

'I hope not. I like her much better this way,' said Clementine.

The children reached the stream where a lovely little stone bridge spanned the banks.

'The sheep are down there,' said Poppy, pointing ahead. Some of the sheep were grazing and others were lying on the grass. In among the mature animals there were lots of lambs.

'Well, have a look, children,' Mrs Bottomley instructed, 'there are the lambs.'

'You can't even see them,' Joshua whined. 'They're too far away.'

'Yes,' Aunt Violet agreed. 'Do you think we can get a little bit closer, Poppy?'

The child nodded. 'Yes, but I don't think we'll be able to touch them.'

'Right, come along then, children,' Aunt

Violet said and began to walk further into the paddock.

'I think we should be getting back soon, Miss Appleby,' Mrs Bottomley declared.

'Nonsense, woman. We've been gone all of fifteen minutes. Unless the Bauers have a supercharged barbecue, those sausages will need a little longer yet.' Aunt Violet shook her head and kept walking.

Clementine and Sophie looked at each other and giggled. It was funny to hear a grown-up talk back to Mrs Bottomley.

Up close, the children could see lots of lambs gambolling about. The little creatures would run quickly past their mothers, as if to show them how steady they were on their feet, then become overwhelmed with shyness and race back for protection.

Poppy warned the group that sometimes the mothers were very bossy and they shouldn't get too close. For the first few minutes everyone had a lovely time watching. Unfortunately that didn't last long.

Joshua had his eye on a tiny lamb. He was determined to catch it and show everyone how clever he was. The boy crept up on the little creature and made a lunge. It skipped out of his grasp and ran towards its mother. Joshua landed on the soft grass, a huge grin on his face.

'Come back here,' he growled, and jumped to his feet.

Mrs Bottomley turned and saw the lad chasing after the lamb. 'Joshua Tribble, stop that at once,' she shouted.

But Mrs Bottomley's shouting only seemed to make the other children excited. Angus took off after another lamb, then Eddie Whipple got in on the act too.

Soon some of the girls joined in the game until sheep, lambs and children scattered over the field like a bag of marbles spilled onto a concrete floor.

Poppy shouted at them to stop. Mrs Bottomley charged through a brambly hedge after Joshua. Aunt Violet had grabbed Angus's collar and was trying to keep a grip on him when Mrs Bottomley began to wail. Clementine and Sophie, who had been standing under one of the oak trees and wondering what was going to happen next, watched wide-eyed as Mrs Bottomley flew out of the hedge with a giant white goose honking and hissing after her.

'Eloise!' Poppy called. 'Leave Mrs Bottomley alone.'

But the goose was not about to stop. Mrs Bottomley wobbled on her feet as she tried to fend off the snapping beak.

'Oh, for heaven's sake, woman. It's a goose, not a charging bull,' chided Aunt Violet. She dropped Angus like a stone and hurried after Mrs Bottomley.

The children all stopped their running about and watched Aunt Violet chasing the goose that was chasing Mrs Bottomley. Joshua began to laugh. Angus did too and soon the whole class was in fits as the two old women and the goose disappeared through the hedge again.

'Where are they?' Angus asked after the trio had been gone a while.

'I'll go and look,' Poppy called.

'I'm coming too,' Angus said.

Astrid's brows knotted together fiercely. 'No, we should all stay here.'

'You're not the boss of us,' Joshua said.

Ella, a tiny girl with long blonde plaits, began to cry. 'Where's Mrs Bottomley?' she sniffled.

Some of the other children were beginning to get upset too. They realised they were alone in the field and the two adults looking after them had vanished.

Poppy grabbed Clementine's hand and together they ran to the edge of the field and scanned the paddock beyond the hedge.

'Where did they go?' Clementine asked as she looked into the empty stretch of green.

'I don't know.' Poppy looked up and down. It seemed the women and the goose had disappeared into thin air.

'What should we do?' Clementine asked.

'We should go and get Daddy,' Poppy declared.

Clementine and Poppy raced back to the oak tree, where the rest of the class was standing.

'Where are they?' Angus asked.

Poppy shrugged.

'I'm going to look,' Joshua declared. 'Because I'm a proper explorer. Girls aren't. They're dumb.'

'We are not,' Clementine said. 'And we're just as good at exploring as you are.'

'Are not,' Joshua spat back.

'We are so,' Clementine shouted at him. She could feel the red rising on her neck.

'Why don't we split up?' Astrid suggested. 'I can take anyone who wants to go back, and Poppy can take anyone who wants to search.'

It sounded reasonable enough to Clementine. She was keen to find Aunt Violet. She didn't think her mummy would be very happy if she lost her, although Uncle Digby probably wouldn't mind.

'Who wants to go with Poppy?' Astrid asked.

Clementine, Sophie, Angus and Joshua put up their hands.

'Who wants to go back?'

A small sea of hands shot into the air.

'I'm starving,' Eddie Whipple groaned.

'Yeah, me too,' said Lester.

'I'll tell your dad where you are, Poppy,' said Astrid. 'Come on then.' She beckoned to the children and began to lead the group back across the field. The sheep and their lambs had all relocated to a quiet spot much further down the paddock.

'Thanks,' Poppy called after her. She turned to the four intrepid adventurers who had stayed behind. 'Now, you have to listen to me because I know everywhere on the farm and I don't want anyone else to get lost.'

'Boring,' Joshua said.

'You can go back with the others if you're going to say that,' Poppy snapped.

'You can't make me,' Joshua said.

'But I will,' Angus growled. He was growing impatient and wanted to find his missing grandmother.

Joshua rolled his eyes.

'We have to stay together,' Poppy said. 'Come on, let's go.'

GONE

Astrid led the rest of the children back to the farmhouse, where the smell of barbecued sausages filled the air.

Lily Bauer looked up from where she was cutting bread rolls in half to see the children trooping into the back garden.

'Hello there. What have you done with Mrs Bottomley?' Lily asked.

'She's gone,' Eddie Whipple said.

Lily frowned. 'What do you mean?'

Astrid spoke up. 'Mrs Bottomley and Clementine's great-aunt disappeared.'

'Disappeared?' said Sophie Rousseau's mother anxiously. She was looking around the group of children and noticed that her own daughter and her friends were missing too.

'Well, we went to see the lambs and then Mrs Bottomley got chased by a goose. It was very angry. Then Clementine's great-aunt chased the goose and they all disappeared,' Astrid explained.

Lily Bauer looked at Odette Rousseau in alarm. 'And where's Poppy?'

'And Sophie?' Mrs Rousseau added.

'Poppy said that she knows everywhere on the farm so she's gone to look for them with Sophie and Clementine, and Joshua and Angus too,' said Astrid.

Lily didn't like the sound of this at all. It was bad enough that no one had located Granny Bert yet, but now Mrs Bottomley and Aunt Violet were missing too, and the children had formed a search party. She knew that Poppy was reliable but Angus and Joshua out there could spell trouble.

'Heinrich, I think you should go and find the children,' Lily suggested as her husband lifted the last of the sausages from the barbecue plate. 'We can get lunch organised for this lot.'

Her husband nodded.

Mr Tribble offered to go too, seeing as Joshua was with them.

Meanwhile, out in the field, Poppy decided that they should head towards the edge of the woods, which was the direction they had last seen Mrs Bottomley and Aunt Violet running.

'They can't be too far,' she said as the five children trooped along.

They came to a stone wall. It wasn't especially high but would have presented a challenge for most five-year-olds.

'How are we supposed to get over that?' Sophie asked.

'Me and Angus can do it,' Joshua bragged. 'Because we're commandos.'

'No you're not,' Sophie said. 'You're little boys.'

'It's okay.' Poppy pointed further along. 'There's a stile.'

'I'm going first.' Joshua raced ahead to where the little ladder straddled the wall. He rushed up and then jumped off the other side.

'Pooh!' he yelled.

'What's the matter now?' Poppy asked. She clambered up the ladder and stood on the top rung. Joshua had landed smack bang in the middle of a cow pat.

Sophie scurried up the ladder next. She held her nose and said, 'That's disgusting.' The two girls giggled.

'You're disgusting.' Joshua hissed and pulled a face.

Angus and Clementine joined the others on the far side of the wall and the five children carried on walking.

'Do you really think they could have come this far?' Clementine asked. She noticed that beyond the field there was thick woodland.

'We can go back if you like,' Poppy said. She was surprised that Aunt Violet and Mrs Bottomley hadn't reappeared.

Clementine shook her head. 'I don't want Aunt Violet to be lost.' She never thought she'd say it, but it was true.

IN A FLAP

The goose called Eloise had chased Mrs Bottomley over a wall and deep into the woods. Aunt Violet followed, waving her arms about and yelling at the white bird.

Mrs Bottomley stumbled and fell backwards and the goose seized her opportunity. She leapt onto the woman's chest. Aunt Violet couldn't believe what she was seeing.

Mrs Bottomley flapped her arms at the creature and screamed.

'Good heavens, get off her.' Aunt Violet

pushed against the goose's sizable rump. Eloise turned and snapped at Aunt Violet, who retreated. The creature turned her attention back to Mrs Bottomley.

Eloise thrust her beak forward and grabbed hold of the shiny silver whistle around the teacher's neck. She pulled at the cord.

'It's strangling me,' Mrs Bottomley wailed.

'Give it to her,' said Aunt Violet.

'What?'

'The whistle, woman. She's after the whistle.' Aunt Violet knelt beside Mrs Bottomley's head and pulled the cord from around her neck. She then played tug-of-war with the goose, who still had the whistle firmly in her beak.

'Why, you beastly creature!' Aunt Violet pulled one way and the goose pulled the other. 'Have your way then!'

As soon as Aunt Violet let go of the whistle, the creature turned and waddled off at lightning pace into the woods.

Ethel Bottomley sat up. She exhaled loudly but didn't seem to be able to find any words.

Aunt Violet was similarly dumbstruck.

The two sat in silence for several minutes.

'Well, that was unexpected,' Aunt Violet said, looking distastefully at the brown marks on her white suit.

'I . . . I think you saved my life, Miss Appleby,' Mrs Bottomley stammered.

'Well, I wouldn't go that far,' Aunt Violet replied. 'But you were in a bit of trouble there.'

A tear fell onto Mrs Bottomley's cheek.

'Are you all right?' Aunt Violet offered her hand and pulled the woman to her feet.

'I think it's just all a bit of a shock.' Mrs Bottomley began to cry.

'Come now, Mrs Bottomley,' Aunt Violet soothed.

Without warning, Ethel Bottomley launched herself at Aunt Violet and hugged her tightly. 'Thank you, Miss Appleby. Thank you,' she sobbed.

Violet Appleby stood rigid for a few moments, wondering what she should do. Then she did the only thing possible and hugged Ethel Bottomley right back.

Seconds later, the women separated and Mrs Bottomley sniffed loudly. 'Where are we?' she asked.

'I don't know.' Aunt Violet looked around under the gloomy canopy of trees. Up ahead she spied a stone wall and a stile leading to an open field. 'I think perhaps we should go that way.'

Mrs Bottomley hobbled along beside her and together they somehow managed to get up and over the stile and into the meadow.

Aunt Violet peered into the afternoon sun. 'I think there's a stream down there. Perhaps it's the one we crossed earlier.'

'I don't know if I can walk much further,' Mrs Bottomley whimpered. Her bunions were aching and she had two enormous blisters on her heels.

The ladies ambled on until they reached an enormous fir tree amid a grove of trees. The dappled light danced around its branches, which scooped towards the ground.

Something caught Aunt Violet's eye. She peered through the foliage. 'Goodness me!'

She lifted the branch and disappeared through the other side.

'Please don't leave me behind,' Mrs Bottomley wailed.

'I'm coming back for you.' Aunt Violet held the branch up and Mrs Bottomley followed her.

'What is this place?' Mrs Bottomley said as she looked about. There was an old kitchen cabinet with a sink, a pine dresser full of china and even a chandelier hanging from one of the branches overhead.

Two green armchairs faced away from them, towards a mock fireplace, and there was a round pine table and four chairs set up as if someone was expected for afternoon tea.

'What do you think it is?' Mrs Bottomley whispered. 'You don't think anyone lives here, do you?'

Aunt Violet smiled and shook her head. 'Of course not. It's a cubbyhouse.'

A silver head peered around the side of one of the armchairs. 'Oh, hello there, dears. I've been expecting you.'

Aunt Violet and Mrs Bottomley spun around. 'Who are you?' they asked in unison.

Heinrich Bauer and Mr Tribble set off on foot to locate the children and lost ladies. Mr Greening had telephoned a few minutes before they left to say that there was no sign of Granny Bert in the village either.

'This is not quite the day I had planned,' Heinrich frowned.

'No, but at least it will be one the children will remember,' Mr Tribble replied cheerily. 'Surely they can't be too far. Besides, there's nothing especially dangerous out here, is there?'

Heinrich began to shake his head then stopped. He thought for a moment. 'Well, apart from the geese, perhaps there is something else.'

'What is it?' Mr Tribble asked.

'I forgot about Ramon,' Heinrich replied.

'Who's Ramon?'

Heinrich gulped. 'He's our ram and I'm afraid he's not very fond of children.'

'He's only a sheep. Surely he couldn't do that much damage,' Mr Tribble replied. 'Where is he?'

'He's in the far meadow just this side of the woods. I moved him yesterday, so Poppy would have no idea that he's there. And you're wrong about Ramon. I've seen him flatten three grown men, myself included. Come on, Mr Tribble, we need to get to him before anyone else does.'

The two men jogged into the long meadow and across the stone bridge over the stream. They looked up and down the length of the field and raced towards the far meadow and the woods beyond.

RAMMED

oppy, Clementine, Sophie and the two boys walked in single file across the far meadow towards the fence.

'What's that?' Joshua looked around just in time to see a huge woolly beast charging towards them.

The other children stopped and looked too.

'Oh my goodness,' Poppy yelled. 'It's Ramon. RUN!'

The children took off as fast as they could. But Ramon was speedy for a sheep. He put his

head down and raced towards them, bleating loudly.

Poppy and Sophie reached the stone wall and scrambled up using the rocks as footholds. Clementine tripped on a stone in the grass and was sent sprawling.

Angus and Joshua were behind her. Joshua kept running but Angus stopped to see if she was all right.

'Come on,' the boy said and grabbed Clemmie's arm.

'My knee hurts,' she whimpered.

Ramon was getting closer and closer.

'Run, Clemmie, run!' Poppy called. Joshua reached the wall and was trying to climb, but his foot kept slipping back.

'Help! He's gonna eat me,' the boy wailed.

Clementine and Angus reached the wall too. Angus scrambled up first and then hauled Clemmie up behind him.

Ramon was flying towards Joshua when all of a sudden the beast pulled up just short of the boy. The ram sniffed. He pawed at the ground and bleated loudly.

'What's he doing?' Angus asked, wondering if he was about to toss Joshua over the wall.

'Joshua, have you got any food in your pockets?' Poppy asked.

Joshua shook his head. Then he remembered he'd stolen an extra brownie at morning tea time. 'Maybe,' he said. He reached into his pocket. 'I've got this.' The brownie was a lot flatter than when he'd shoved it in there.

'Give it to him,' Poppy yelled. 'Hold your hand out flat and give it to him.'

'To the *sheep*?' Joshua asked, frowning.

'Yes, to Ramon. He loves chocolate. As soon as he takes it, climb onto the wall,' the girl replied.

Joshua wondered what sort of sheep ate chocolate. He held out the squished cake and waited. Ramon sniffed his hand then licked his palm.

'That tickles,' the boy giggled.

Ramon began to nibble at the brownie. Then he chewed it for a minute or so before gulping it down. Joshua had just enough time to clamber onto the top of the stone wall.

'Dumb sheep,' Joshua said. 'He's not scary.'

Ramon then charged forward and head-butted the wall with such force that the stones on top shook. Joshua wobbled and just managed to stay upright.

'Yes, he is.' The boy raced along the wall to the stile, where his friends were waiting. 'He could have killed me.'

'Yeah, but he didn't,' Angus replied. He turned to Clementine. 'Your knee's bleeding. Here, have this.' Angus pulled a clean white handkerchief from his pocket and handed it to Clemmie, who mopped up the blood.

'Thank you, Angus,' she said. 'You saved me from that crazy sheep.'

Angus smiled. 'It was nothing.'

'Come on.' Joshua jumped down from the wall. 'Let's go and find those stupid old ladies.'

Angus glared at the boy. Poppy did too.

A VERY STRANGE
TEA PARTY

Poppy led the children along the edge of the woods.

'Mrs Bottomley!' Sophie called.

'Aunt Violet, where are you?' Clementine called too.

The children were making as much noise as they possibly could, but there was still no reply.

'I wonder why Mrs Bottomley doesn't just blow her whistle,' Clementine said. 'Then we could find them.'

'I'm hungry,' Joshua grumbled. 'I want my brownie back.'

'You shouldn't have had it in the first place,' Sophie said. 'But it's lucky you did, or you'd probably have a very sore bottom right now.'

The other children giggled.

'Let's go home and see if they've turned up there,' said Poppy. 'I know a shortcut.'

'It better not be anywhere near that sheep again,' warned Joshua.

Poppy shook her head. 'It's not.'

The children all agreed. They had no idea what time it was but it was quite likely the adults would be getting worried about them by now.

They climbed up and over another stile and sped across an open field. Poppy assured everyone that Ramon couldn't get near them, but they decided to go as quickly as they could just to be on the safe side.

The children crossed into the far end of the long meadow.

'Shh, what's that noise?' Clementine said.

'I can't hear anything except the lambs and some ducks,' Sophie replied.

Clemmie listened more closely. 'No, there's something else.'

The children entered a grove of trees. The sound of muffled laughter was unmistakable.

'It's coming from over there,' called Clemmie. She ran towards the giant fir tree.

'That's our cubby,' said Poppy, and chased after her. She pulled back the branch that shielded the entry and the children followed her inside. They couldn't believe their eyes.

'Nan?' Angus exclaimed.

'Aunt Violet, what are you doing here?' Clementine asked.

Poppy's jaw dropped. 'Granny Bert!'

The three elderly women were sitting around the pine kitchen table, laughing like hyenas.

The children noticed the old chipped teacups and saucers on the table. They were completely dry.

Aunt Violet turned and smiled at the group. 'Oh, thank heavens.'

'We're saved!' said Mrs Bottomley, clasping her hands together.

Granny Bert frowned. 'You didn't tell me you'd invited more guests.'

'Granny, it's me, Poppy.' The girl walked over and stood in front of the woman.

'Poppy, of course I know it's you. Do you think I'm losing my marbles?' Granny Bert said with a broad grin.

The children didn't know what to think.

'What are you doing here?' Angus asked.

'We found this place by accident and Mrs Rumble was here already, so we thought we'd just sit and have a rest before we tried to find our way back to the house. I'm afraid your grandmother has some terrible blisters,' Aunt Violet explained.

'But what were you laughing about?' Clementine asked.

'What were we laughing about?' Aunt Violet looked at the other ladies, who shrugged.

'Do we need to have a reason to laugh?' Mrs Bottomley asked. 'I think young people these days take life far too seriously.'

Aunt Violet began to giggle. Granny Bert did too. Mrs Bottomley roared with laughter.

The children didn't understand any of it.

'Are you going to be friends now?' Clementine asked her great-aunt when the laughter finally died down.

'Friends? With Mrs Bottomley? I can't imagine it, dear. She's a dreadful woman,' Aunt Violet said with a grin.

Clementine gasped. 'Aunt Violet, she's sitting right next to you.'

'Yes, I can see her. I don't think she can see me, though. You know she's blind as a bat and deaf as a beetle.'

The other children gasped too.

Mrs Bottomley's eyes crinkled. 'But that's all right, Clementine, because your great-aunt is quite the rudest woman I've ever met in my life and I wouldn't want to be friends with her either.'

The children all gulped and wondered what was about to happen next.

'Oh, for goodness sake, we're joking. We're pulling your legs.' Aunt Violet nudged Mrs Bottomley, who grinned.

'Miss Appleby saved me from that crazy goose. If it wasn't for her, I'd probably be lying in the field with that giant white monster taking a nap on my belly.' The children looked from one woman to the next, wondering what had happened out there. 'But I do think we should be getting back before Mr Bauer does something ridiculous like call the police. Angus, you can wait here with me and I think you should wait here too, Mrs Rumble,' directed Mrs Bottomley. 'Are you right to go with the children, Miss Appleby?'

Violet Appleby stood up. 'Yes, of course.'

Granny Bert nodded. 'I don't know where Lily got to with that morning tea, but I wish she'd hurry up.'

'Come along, Clementine,' Aunt Violet instructed.

Clemmie walked towards her great-aunt. The woman slipped her hand into Clemmie's and they followed Poppy, Sophie and Joshua out of the cubby.

'There's Daddy,' Poppy shouted. She began to race towards the figure in the distance.

'Aunt Violet, are you really going to be friends with Mrs Bottomley?' Clementine looked up at the woman. Aunt Violet's hair was rumpled and her white suit was a patchwork of brown and green stains.

Aunt Violet smiled. 'Let's just say that sometimes it takes a fiasco to help two stubborn old women understand one another.'

'What's a fiasco?' Clementine had never heard that word before.

'A disaster,' her great-aunt replied. 'And I think today has been just that, don't you?'

Clementine shook her head. 'No, Aunt Violet, I don't think so at all. Angus saved me from Ramon and Joshua saved himself with a chocolate brownie and you saved Mrs Bottomley and made a new friend. So I'd say that today has been just about perfect. Wouldn't you?'

Aunt Violet smoothed her hair and then grinned. 'Perhaps. But you're not to breathe a word of any of this to Pertwhistle or your mother. Do you understand?'

Clementine nodded. Maybe she didn't mind having a secret with Aunt Violet after all.

ANOTHER SECRET

Everyone was relieved when Aunt Violet appeared with the children. Mr Bauer had raced home to get the four-wheel drive and transport Mrs Bottomley and Granny Bert back to the farmhouse. Lily found some bandaids for Mrs Bottomley's blisters and insisted that the woman sit in the garden to rest.

Although lunch was late for some, it was delicious and much appreciated. After everyone had eaten, Aunt Violet took charge and the children had a wonderful time identifying and pulling up some vegetables, and meeting a couple of the horses which Max, the stablehand at Highton Hall, brought down especially.

'I think it's almost time to go,' said Aunt Violet. She could hear the rattle of the bus coming down the lane. 'Gather up your bags children and let's go and meet Mr Stubbs, shall we?'

Mrs Bottomley appeared and insisted that everyone line up so she could call the roll.

Aunt Violet let her go. It was still her excursion after all, and at least she no longer had that dreadful whistle.

'Where's Joshua Tribble?' Mrs Bottomley asked, looking straight at the boy's father.

'He's just gone to the toilet,' Mr Tribble replied.

'Well, go and get him,' Mrs Bottomley demanded. 'We need to get moving.' Mrs Bottomley had had quite enough adventures for one day – and although it was tempting to leave the boy behind, she could only imagine what Miss Critchley would have to say about that.

'Good day, Ethel?' Bernie Stubbs asked as Mrs Bottomley boarded the bus.

'Yes, Mr Stubbs. A surprisingly good day,' the woman replied.

He grinned. 'I do like to hear that.'

The children bade farewell to Mr and Mrs Bauer, Poppy and Granny Bert, and thanked them loudly for a wonderful day.

'So what do you think of life on a farm?' Mr Tribble asked his son as they sat together in the middle of the bus.

'It's okay,' said Joshua. 'But I don't like sheep much.'

Clementine was sitting in the front seat next to Aunt Violet. As the bus lurched forward, bumping along the narrow country lane, she was surprised to see Eloise the goose waddling between two of the sheds with what looked like Mrs Bottomley's shiny silver whistle around her neck.

She turned to her great-aunt. 'Did you see that?'

Aunt Violet raised her eyebrows and smiled. 'Let's just hope she doesn't learn how to use it. Can I tell you a secret, Clementine?'

Clementine looked at her great-aunt cautiously. She already had the secret of the crystal vase to worry about, and not telling about today's adventure with Mrs Bottomley and Eloise. 'Okay.'

The old woman whispered, 'I think I actually enjoyed myself at the farm. It was a most unpredictable outing.'

Clementine looked at her in shock. 'That's the secret?'

Aunt Violet nodded.

Clementine leaned in and cuddled her. 'Thank you, Aunt Violet.'

'Whatever for?' her great-aunt asked.

Clementine grinned. 'For being unpredictable too.'

CAST OF CHARACTERS

The Appleby household

Clementine Rose Appleby	Five-year-old daughter of Lady Clarissa
Lavender	Clemmie's teacup pig
Lady Clarissa Appleby	Clementine's mother and the owner of Penberthy House
Digby Pertwhistle	Butler at Penberthy House
Aunt Violet Appleby	Clementine's grandfather's sister

Pharaoh	Aunt Violet's beloved sphynx cat

School staff and students

Miss Arabella Critchley	Head teacher at Ellery Prep
Mrs Ethel Bottomley	Teacher at Ellery Prep
Sophie Rousseau	Clementine's best friend – also five years old
Poppy Bauer	Clementine's good friend – also five years old
Angus Archibald	Kindergarten boy
Joshua Tribble	Naughty friend of Angus's
Astrid	Clever kindergarten girl
Eddie Whipple, Lester, Ella	Kindergarten classmates

Others

Odette Rousseau	Sophie's mother
Mr Tribble	Joshua's father

Heinrich Bauer	Poppy's father, manages the farm at Highton Hall
Lily Bauer	Poppy's mother, works on the farm and at Highton Hall
Granny Bert (Albertine	Elderly lady, lives next to the farm in Rose Rumble) Cottage
Daisy Rumble	Granny Bert's granddaughter, also lives at Rose Cottage
Bernie Stubbs	Bus driver

CLEMENTINE ROSE
ROSE
and the Seaside Escape

Jacqueline Harvey

RANDOM HOUSE AUSTRALIA

For Ian, who makes me laugh,
and for Nana and Grandad,
and Mum and Dad, who gave me
many great memories of seaside escapes

A MINOR DELAY

Clementine Rose leaned between the front seats of Uncle Digby's ancient Morris Minor. She looked up at her great-aunt Violet, who had insisted on travelling in the front.

'Is it . . .' Clementine paused. 'Is it an old person?' she asked with a frown.

Aunt Violet turned and curled her lip. 'Who are you calling old? Unless you mean him.' She glanced at Digby Pertwhistle, who was in the driver's seat.

Clementine shook her head. 'No.'

Aunt Violet smiled smugly.

'I meant both of you,' Clementine said.

The grin slid from the woman's lips.

Clementine's mother, Lady Clarissa, was wedged in the back seat with Lavender and Clementine. Before Aunt Violet could erupt, she called out. 'Is it the owl on Uncle Digby's key ring?'

'Yes, it is. Thank goodness that's over,' Aunt Violet harrumphed. 'I've had quite enough of I Spy for one day.'

'But it's Mummy's turn,' said Clementine.

'Godfathers! Can't you just look at the scenery, Clementine?' Aunt Violet protested.

Clementine wrinkled her nose.

The little car puttered to the top of another rise. They had been driving for a couple of hours now. They had passed green fields dotted with oak trees and sheep, lush forests, and now the landscape had opened up again.

'Look!' Clementine shouted, bouncing up and down in her seat.

'Yes, yes, we can all see it,' said Aunt Violet. But even she couldn't suppress the start of a smile.

The ocean spread out before them, twinkling in the afternoon sun. There was a pretty village dotted with whitewashed houses and a perfect crescent beach tucked in between a little harbour and a rocky headland. Further around, the green hills looked as if they rolled all the way to the sandy shore.

'It's beautiful,' Clementine gasped.

'It certainly is,' said Digby. 'And just as I remember it from when I was a boy.'

'I'm surprised you can recall anything that far back,' Aunt Violet teased.

'Don't you worry, Miss Appleby. I have a mind like a steel trap.' Digby tapped his left temple and winked in the old woman's direction.

Aunt Violet rolled her eyes.

'Can we go to the beach this afternoon?' Clementine asked.

'Mmm, I think perhaps we should get settled and then take a walk around the village.

Remember, we've got a whole week, Clemmie,' her mother replied.

'Do you really think those builders will have the new roof on in a week?' Aunt Violet asked. 'They looked an untrustworthy lot, if you ask me.'

'Aunt Violet, I've known Mr Hubbard since I was a little girl and I thought you'd much rather have a holiday by the sea than be woken by builders in the rafters above your bed,' Clarissa replied.

Aunt Violet sighed. 'Yes, yes, you've made your point. In fact, I don't know why we couldn't have stayed for two weeks. One seems a bit stingy, really.'

'One is all I could afford,' Lady Clarissa reminded her aunt.

'I suppose it's for the best. I couldn't bear to leave Pharaoh for longer. I do hope that cat of Mrs Mogg's doesn't lead the dear boy astray,' said Aunt Violet. 'I've heard Claws is a bit of a traveller too.'

Pharaoh was Aunt Violet's sphynx cat.

He was quite possibly the strangest creature Clementine had ever seen, all wrinkly and hairless. But he and Clementine's teacup pig, Lavender, had fallen madly in love, and Clementine adored him too. The only problem was that Pharaoh had a terrible habit of escaping. Aunt Violet had thought about taking him along for the week but, after he'd gone missing for an entire day yet again, she decided it was safer to leave him with the local shopkeeper. Mrs Mogg vowed to keep him under lock and key.

Penberthy House had been in need of a new roof for some time but a recent heavy downpour confirmed that it could wait no longer. Clementine, her mother, Uncle Digby and even Aunt Violet couldn't find enough buckets to collect the drips. As luck would have it, Lady Clarissa had hosted two beautiful weddings in recent months, which had given her enough money to have the roof replaced, as well as a few other minor repairs. The holiday was a lovely bonus.

'What will our hotel be like?' Clementine asked.

'Watertight, I hope,' Aunt Violet smirked.

'Of course it will be,' Clarissa laughed. 'And it's a guesthouse, not a hotel. So I imagine it will be almost like staying with friends. Mrs Dent sounded lovely on the telephone.'

'What's the difference between a guesthouse and a hotel, Mummy?' Clementine asked.

'Not much, darling. It will just be a lot cosier,' Clarissa replied.

Digby Pertwhistle crunched the gears as the little car coughed and sputtered on the narrow road to the village. There was one last hill before they would begin their descent.

Aunt Violet shuddered at the noise. 'I don't see why we couldn't have taken my car.'

Digby wrestled the gears again. 'I think that had something to do with you not getting the registration paid in time.'

Aunt Violet pursed her lips and went strangely quiet.

Suddenly there was a loud bang and the little car slowed down. Digby just managed to steer it off the road and onto the grass verge before it rolled to a halt.

'Uh-oh.' Clementine looked at her mother. 'That didn't sound good.'

'Wonderful,' Aunt Violet grouched. 'I might have guessed something like this would happen.'

Digby opened the door and walked to the front of the car. He lifted the bonnet and thick steam poured from the engine bay.

'You stay here, darling,' said Lady Clarissa before she hopped out to join him.

Aunt Violet wound down the window. 'Hurry up, Pertwhistle. I'm dying of thirst in here!'

Clementine leaned forward again. 'Are you excited?' she asked her great-aunt.

'About what? The prospect of having to walk the last couple of miles to the village or the fact that we'll be staying in a fleapit of a guesthouse that will be altogether too hot and probably smell like boiled cabbages.'

Clementine frowned. 'I meant are you excited about having a holiday by the sea.' She had no idea why her great-aunt thought the house would smell like cabbages. Penberthy House never did.

'I might be, if we ever get there,' the woman replied.

Clementine thought Aunt Violet was a complicated person. The two of them hadn't exactly hit it off when they first met and they'd certainly had their fair share of run-ins. But more recently the woman had seemed to soften a little, although she was still the grumpiest person Clemmie knew.

'Do you want to hear a poem?' Clementine asked.

'No, not particularly,' Aunt Violet replied, craning her neck to see what was going on in front of the car.

'But it's about you,' Clementine said.

'About me?' Aunt Violet eyed the girl suspiciously.

Clementine nodded. 'It's a limerick. Uncle

Digby taught me how to do them. I've just made up one about you in my head.'

'Well, get on with it,' said Aunt Violet.

Clementine frowned in confusion. 'But . . . you said you didn't want to hear it.'

'And now I've changed my mind.'

Clementine began:

'There once was a lady called Vi
Who accidentally swallowed a fly
It tickled and buzzed
And prickled and fuzzed
'Til she coughed it back into the sky.'

Clementine leaned forward to watch her great-aunt's reaction. 'Did you like it?'

Violet Appleby's lips quivered. 'As a matter of fact, Clementine, I thought it was rather . . . clever.' The old woman's mouth stretched into a smile.

'Uncle Digby told me that Vi was short for Violet, because sometimes he calls you that. So I rhymed "Vi" with "fly",' the girl said with a grin.

'Well, I certainly hope I won't be swallowing any flies on this holiday,' said Aunt Violet. 'And Pertwhistle can stop calling me Vi behind my back too – the cheek of him.' She stuck her head out of the window. 'For heaven's sake, what's taking so long?'

A TIGHT SQUEEZE

Just as Aunt Violet was grouching and gasping, a beaten-up tow truck with faded letters on the side pulled off the road ahead of them. A man of sizable proportions slid down from the driver's seat.

He doffed his pork-pie hat towards Lady Clarissa and Uncle Digby. 'Looks like you could do with a hand.'

Lady Clarissa beamed at him. 'Oh, your timing couldn't be better.'

'It's the fan belt,' said Digby, as he held

up the rubbery remains. 'And the old girl's overheated too.'

The man nodded. 'Don't think I have one your size in the truck.'

'We're going to Endersley-on-Sea,' Lady Clarissa explained. 'We could almost walk from here.'

Aunt Violet opened the passenger door and stalked around to the front of the car. 'Well, you could but I'm certainly not!'

The man doffed his hat towards Aunt Violet. 'I can give you a tow, but you'll all have to squash in with me, I'm afraid,' he explained.

Violet Appleby looked at the truck and shuddered. 'I'm not going in that thing.'

'I can send the taxi back for you if you'd prefer.' The man grinned. 'But I know Old Parky's been a bit busy so it might take a while for him to get here. He's the only one in the village.'

Clementine hopped out of the car too.

'Hello there, young lady,' the man said and smiled at her.

'Hello. Are you going to fix our car?' she asked.

'I will when we get it to my workshop. Is anyone else in there?' He already thought there was a surprising number of passengers for such a small vehicle.

'Only Lavender,' Clemmie replied.

Mr Phipps frowned.

'She's my teacup pig. She's not very big at all.' Clementine ran to the back door of the car and retrieved her pet. 'Here she is.'

Lenny tickled the little creature and said, 'Well, it's going to be a tight squeeze, but I'm sure we can all fit in.'

Clementine was almost bursting at the thought of riding in the front of a tow truck.

'Wait until I tell Angus that we got to go in a proper truck,' she said, dancing about.

'If we'd driven a proper car, we wouldn't be going anywhere near that thing you're calling a truck,' Aunt Violet muttered.

Lady Clarissa ignored her. 'Thank you very much, Mr . . .?' She hesitated, waiting for the man to introduce himself.

'The name's Lenny, Lenny Phipps.'

Within a couple of minutes, the little Morris Minor was hooked up to the back of the truck and the family was jammed in along the bench seat. Clementine sat on her mother's lap nursing Lavender, with Aunt Violet beside her next to Mr Phipps. Uncle Digby was squeezed in by the passenger door. With some fiddling about, everyone was strapped in, and soon they were on their way.

WELCOME

I t wasn't long before Mr Phipps pulled up
outside a pretty whitewashed townhouse
in the middle of the village. It was right
opposite the harbour, three storeys high
with wide bay windows. Out the front was a
small garden with neatly clipped hedges and
a colourful bed of petunias.

'Is that where we're staying?' Clementine
asked. She tried to sound out the name on the
front gate. 'En-der-sley-on-Sea Guesthouse.'

Clarissa nodded. 'This is it.'

Digby studied the building. 'I have a feeling I might have stayed here when I was a boy.'

'I hope they've updated things since then,' said Aunt Violet, 'or we might as well have stayed at home and dodged the builders.'

Lenny Phipps and Digby Pertwhistle opened the truck's doors. Aunt Violet and Lady Clarissa breathed out. Clementine gave a big sigh and Lavender grunted loudly.

'I'll help you with your things,' Mr Phipps offered as he hopped out and walked around to Digby's little car.

Digby poked his head back inside the cabin. 'Clarissa, dear, why don't you take everyone inside and I'll sort the rest.'

Lady Clarissa nodded.

'I hope they make a decent cup of tea,' Aunt Violet grumbled. 'I'm parched.'

Clementine picked up Lavender and held her tight. The tiny pig was wearing her sparkly red collar and lead.

'I love this place already,' said Clementine.

Her mother looked at her. 'Already?'

'Yes, because I don't think there are many guesthouses where you can bring pigs.'

Clementine was right about that. Lady Clarissa had called more than a dozen guesthouses and hotels along the coast before she had found this one. The owner, Mrs Dent, said she was happy to have four-legged guests as long as they behaved themselves and were house-trained. Clarissa had mentioned that Lavender was a teacup pig, expecting the woman to change her mind. But Mrs Dent had been delighted by the idea.

The ladies and Clementine made their way through the front gate as Lenny Phipps waved goodbye to them.

Clementine followed her mother into the front hall. There was a small reception desk with a bell, which Clarissa let Clementine ring.

A voice tinkled from down the hallway. 'Hello, hello?'

A woman appeared. She was short and round, with a tummy that looked as soft as a pillow. She reminded Clementine of Mrs Mogg.

'Hello,' said Lady Clarissa. 'You must be Mrs Dent.'

'I am indeed, dear. Rosamund Dent at your service. And you must be Clarissa Appleby.'

Clementine liked Mrs Dent's rosy cheeks and the way her eyes sparkled when she spoke.

'Oh my goodness, is that little Lavender?' She rushed towards Clementine, who was nursing the animal, and leaned down to nuzzle her face against the tiny pig.

Lavender grunted and snuggled Mrs Dent back.

'Oh, she's precious.' Mrs Dent rubbed Lavender's head.

Clementine smiled. 'She likes you.'

'This is my daughter, Clementine, and my aunt, Violet Appleby,' Lady Clarissa explained.

'Good afternoon,' said Aunt Violet.

'Hello,' said Clementine. 'Uncle Digby is outside with Mr Phipps. Our car broke down so we had to get it towed.'

'Oh, dear me, what a dreadful way to start a holiday,' said the old woman.

'Yes, you can't imagine –' Aunt Violet began to grizzle. She was all set to continue when Mrs Dent stopped her in her tracks.

'How about I show you to your rooms and then I'll pop the kettle on. And I hope you like strawberry sponge cake.'

'Yes, please!' Clementine clapped her hands together.

'Do you have a full house at the moment?' Lady Clarissa asked as the woman walked around the reception desk.

'No, dear, there's just your group, and my grandchildren, who are visiting. Their parents have gone away for a couple of weeks, so they're all mine. You picked a good time to come – things will get much busier towards the end of the month.'

Clementine's eyes lit up. 'How old are your grandchildren?'

'Freddy is almost eight and his sister Della is ten,' Mrs Dent replied. 'And I'm sure they will love having an extra playmate for the holidays. I'm a bit boring, you see. I'm good with making cakes and reading stories but when it comes to the beach, I'm not much fun at all.'

'Like Aunt Violet,' Clementine replied. 'She's good at stories too, but I don't think she'll take me swimming.'

Violet peered down at the child. 'Says who?'

'Well, you said that you don't like sand, and the beach is covered in it,' Clementine explained.

Aunt Violet raised her eyebrows. 'We'll see about that.'

Mrs Dent picked up three keys on large wooden key rings and handed them to Lady Clarissa. 'Mr Pertwhistle and Miss Appleby have their own rooms and there's another for you and Clementine.'

'Perfect,' said Lady Clarissa.

'I've put you all together on the first floor.'

Clementine looked around her. The house was freshly painted, with pretty blue wallpaper and lots of white furniture, but she didn't think it was as lovely as her own home – even with the drips and peeling paint. There were no portraits, either. Clementine thought about the pictures of her long-departed grandparents on the walls in the grand entry at Penberthy House. She hoped they wouldn't be too lonely without her chatting to them and practising her poems.

'Come along, then. I'll take you upstairs,' said Mrs Dent.

'Where are your grandchildren?' Clementine asked as they trooped down the hall.

'They'll be back soon. I sent them to the shop to pick up some more vegetables for dinner.'

Lavender grunted loudly at this.

'Yes, I'm sure you like vegetables too, little one,' Mrs Dent said with a laugh.

Clementine giggled.

A POEM

In no time flat, Uncle Digby had delivered the suitcases to the rooms and everyone had unpacked, ready to start their holiday. Mr Phipps towed Uncle Digby's car to his workshop. It wasn't a bother, as they weren't planning to use the car at all. They wouldn't need to, because the guesthouse was right in the middle of the village, with the beach just across the road.

Downstairs, the sweet smell of freshly baked cakes filled the air and the long dining room table was perfectly laid with fine china and pretty floral napkins.

'Mrs Dent, you really didn't have to go to all this trouble,' Clarissa protested when she saw the room. 'We'd have been just as happy in the kitchen.'

'Oh, my dear, I couldn't do that to you on your first afternoon. But I might from now on, if you really don't mind. I've got a beautiful old table in there – perhaps we can have breakfast and lunch in the kitchen and I'll use the dining room in the evenings,' the old woman suggested.

Clementine thought Mrs Dent had the loveliest smile wrinkles she'd ever seen.

'Well, I know that Clementine and Uncle Digby and I would be very happy with that, and Aunt Violet will just have to get used to it,' said Lady Clarissa firmly.

Aunt Violet appeared in the doorway. 'What will I have to get used to?' She'd changed out of the navy pants-suit she'd worn for travelling and was now in a smart pair of cream trousers with a red silk blouse and matching ballet flats. Clementine thought that she looked very stylish, although perhaps a bit overdressed for a beach holiday.

'I was just saying that Mrs Dent didn't have to go to all this trouble for us. We'd be happy taking tea in the kitchen,' Clarissa said.

'Oh yes, absolutely,' Aunt Violet agreed.

Clarissa was surprised to hear it. So was Clementine, who asked if her great-aunt was feeling all right.

'Yes, of course. A bit thirsty, but I'm fine,' the old woman replied. 'Why do you ask?'

'Well, at home you're always grouching that the guests get to use the dining room and we have to stay in the kitchen,' Clementine explained.

'Just as long as I don't have to do any work for the next week, I don't mind where Mrs Dent feeds us,' Aunt Violet said.

Clementine stared at her, puzzled. 'But you don't do any work at home.'

'I beg your pardon, young lady,' the old woman snapped. 'I'll have you know I'm a very busy person.'

'Usually busy complaining,' said Uncle Digby under his breath.

Aunt Violet spun around and narrowed her eyes. 'I heard that, Pertwhistle.'

'Why don't you all come and have a drink and something to eat?' said Mrs Dent. She winked at Clementine. She could see that her guests were going to keep her entertained.

Digby Pertwhistle helped seat the ladies, as he was used to doing at home. He glanced up at Mrs Dent, and his forehead creased. 'I can't help thinking I've met you before, Mrs Dent.'

She looked up. 'You know, I've been thinking the same thing. You look familiar but I don't recognise your name.'

'Has the house always taken guests?' Digby asked.

The woman shook her head. 'No, my late husband and I bought it as a family home – from my aunt and uncle, actually. They used to come here for holidays. When Hector passed away a few years ago, I turned it into a guesthouse. I couldn't stand rattling around here on my own.'

Digby frowned. There was a memory scratching inside his head.

'So much for that mind like a steel trap, eh, Pertwhistle?' Aunt Violet teased. 'More like a sieve, don't you think?'

Digby grinned. 'Well, as Clementine pointed out earlier, neither of us are spring chickens any more.'

Just as Mrs Dent finished pouring the tea and Lady Clarissa served the cake, the front door banged and there was the sound of feet running down the hallway.

'I think the children are back,' said Mrs Dent. She went to intercept them.

'What have you done with Lavender?' Uncle Digby asked.

'She's having a sleep in her basket,' Clementine said. 'She was 'sausted.'

Clementine took a bite of her sponge cake and picked up the glass of lemonade Mrs Dent had poured for her.

'This is almost as good as Uncle Pierre's cake,' said Clemmie, while munching happily.

Mrs Dent appeared in the doorway with two children. 'I'd like you to meet my granddaughter, Della, and my grandson, Freddy.'

The girl was tall and thin with light-brown hair pulled into a ponytail. She had piercing green eyes and wore green shorts and a pink t-shirt with a glittery heart in the centre. The boy was blond-haired and blue-eyed and, on first glance, looked more like Clementine than his sister.

There was a chorus of hellos from the adults.

'You said she was older,' Della whispered to her grandmother. 'She's just a baby.'

'Della,' Mrs Dent chided.

Clementine looked at the girl. She wore nice clothes but her face seemed the complete opposite of her grandmother's. There was no sparkling and twinkling. Della looked as if she had swallowed something nasty.

'Freddy, Della, aren't you going to say hello to Clementine?' Mrs Dent asked.

'Hello.' Freddy gave a shy smile.

'Hello,' Della said with a pout.

Clementine's tummy twinged. Her mother looked at her and nodded.

'Hello,' Clementine replied.

Mrs Dent set about cutting some more cake for the children and directed them to sit at the other end of the table, near Clementine.

Soon the adults were chatting about this and that and the children were left to their own devices.

'How old are you?' Della asked Clementine with a mouthful of cake.

'I'm five and a half,' the younger girl replied.

Della sighed. 'Granny said that I'd have someone to play with but you're way too young. I only play with people who are seven and over.'

'I can do lots of things a seven-year-old can,' Clementine said hopefully.

'Like what?' Della challenged her.

'I can skip with a rope,' Clementine said.

'Any baby can do that,' Della scoffed.

'I can read lots of hard words and I can make up poems,' Clementine said.

'No, you can't.' Della shook her head. 'Five-year-olds are too stupid to make up poems.'

'That's not true,' Clementine said. She wondered why this girl was so mean and bossy. It seemed strange that her grandmother was about the kindest person Clemmie had met, but Della was crabbier than her teacher, Mrs Bottomley, and Joshua Tribble put together.

'I can make up a poem about you,' Clementine blurted.

Della's eyes narrowed. 'No, you can't.'

'Yes, I can,' Clementine nodded.

'Show me then,' said Della.

Clementine was trying to remember what Uncle Digby had taught her about limericks.

'There once was a girl called Della . . .' Clementine stopped. She was thinking about the next line. It was hard to come up with something that rhymed with that name.

Uncle Digby had half an ear on what was happening and leaned over and whispered something to Clementine.

The child smiled.

'Well, get on with it,' Della said.

Clementine tried again: 'There once was a girl called Della, who was in love with a cute little fella –'

Della glared at Clementine. 'I don't love anybody!'

'But I haven't finished yet.' Clementine felt her bottom lip wobble. She hadn't meant to upset the girl.

'Come on, Freddy. We're going upstairs.' Della pushed back her chair and pinched her brother's arm.

'Ow,' the boy complained.

'Della, why don't you take Clementine with you too?' Mrs Dent suggested.

But the girl raced off. Freddy turned and looked at Clementine. He gave an embarrassed half-smile and scurried from the room.

A fat tear sprouted in the corner of Clementine's eye.

'Are you all right, darling?' her mother asked.

Clementine brushed it away and nodded.

Digby Pertwhistle leaned over and kissed the top of the child's head. 'Don't worry about her, Clemmie. I don't think she appreciates poetry.'

'Did Della say something to upset you?' Mrs Dent asked from her seat at the other end of the table.

'She'd better not have,' Aunt Violet said tersely.

Clementine shook her head. She didn't want to get anyone in trouble, especially not if she had to share the house with them for the next week.

FREDDY

'Shall we go for a walk around the village?' Lady Clarissa asked Clementine as they climbed the stairs to their room.

Clementine nodded. 'Will Aunt Violet and Uncle Digby come too?'

Her mother shook her head. 'Uncle Digby's going to have a lie down and I suspect Aunt Violet might be planning a rest too.'

'Is Uncle Digby all right?' Clemmie's voice was anxious. Since he'd spent time in hospital earlier in the year, she worried a lot about the old man.

'Oh, yes, darling. I think the drive just took it out of him – and having the car break down was a little bit stressful.'

'Especially with Aunt Violet there,' said Clementine.

'Yes, *especially* with Aunt Violet there,' her mother agreed.

The pair walked along the hall to their room at the front of the hotel. It had a beautiful view over the harbour. Aunt Violet's room was even bigger, with a bay window seat. Uncle Digby's room was on the other side of the hall, looking over the back garden.

Lavender appeared to be snoozing in her basket. But as soon as Clementine picked up the sparkly red lead that was hanging on the wardrobe door, the tiny pig scrambled to her feet and danced about at the child's knees.

'Someone's keen to go exploring,' said Lady Clarissa as she grabbed a pink cardigan for Clementine and threw a white jacket around her own shoulders.

Clementine snapped Lavender's lead onto her collar and the trio set off.

Downstairs, they bumped into Mrs Dent, who was balancing a stack of plates from the dining room.

'Have a good walk,' the old woman said with a smile. She carried on into the kitchen.

'Oh, I forgot the camera,' Lady Clarissa said. 'I'll just dash up and get it.'

Clementine was left standing on her own in the entrance hall. 'Mrs Dent's lovely, isn't she, Lavender?' Clementine said to the little pig. 'But I'm not sure about Della. I don't think she likes me.'

The floorboards creaked and Clementine spun around. She saw a face peeking out from one of the doorways. It was Freddy.

The boy's blue eyes widened underneath his mop of blond hair. 'Is that a pig?'

Clementine nodded. 'Her name's Lavender.'

'She's cute,' the boy replied as he took some tentative steps towards them. He knelt down and gave Lavender a rub on the neck.

The little pig repaid him by nibbling his fingers.

'That tickles,' he giggled. 'Is she a piglet?'

'No,' Clementine replied. 'She's a teacup pig.'

'Cool!' said the boy. 'I've never seen one before.'

'Where's your sister?' Clementine asked.

'She's making up a dance,' said Freddy. 'She does that all the time.'

'I love dancing,' Clementine said.

Lady Clarissa walked towards the children. 'Hello, Freddy.'

The lad looked up and smiled. 'Hello. Are you going for a walk?'

Clementine nodded.

'Can I come?'

Clarissa looked at her daughter and raised her eyebrows ever so slightly. Clementine smiled and nodded.

'Yes, of course, but you'll have to ask your grandmother,' Clarissa said.

The boy dashed to the kitchen. He was back in no time, grinning. 'Granny said I could go.'

'What about your sister?' Clarissa asked. 'Do you think she'd like to come as well?'

Freddy shook his head firmly. 'No. She's busy.'

'You can be our tour guide,' Clementine said.

Freddy nodded. 'Can we go now?'

Lady Clarissa thought the lad was awfully eager to get moving. He rushed down the hall and wrenched open the front door.

'Come on, there's a lot to see,' the boy said as he held the door open for Lady Clarissa, Clementine and Lavender.

As Freddy pulled it shut behind him, a shrill voice screeched, 'Freddy, where are you? You're supposed to be helping me with my dance.'

There was the sound of a door slamming and pounding feet on the stairs.

Clementine looked back at the house. 'I think that was your sister.'

'I didn't hear anything,' the boy replied and bounded off down the garden path.

Clementine looked at her mother, who shrugged, and the pair kept walking.

ENDERSLEY~ ON~SEA

F reddy turned out to be a wonderful guide indeed. He introduced Clementine and her mother to Mrs Lee, who owned the village store, and Mr Alessi, the fish and chip shop owner. Mr Alessi's brothers ran a small fleet of fishing boats that were moored in the harbour. Freddy took them past Mr Phipps's workshop, where Uncle Digby's little car was hoisted up high. Lastly, they met Mrs Pink, who owned the bakery and tearooms.

Clementine thought the village was one of

the prettiest she'd ever seen. She loved the whitewashed houses and shops and grand sandstone buildings. Just past the harbour was the beach. On a grassy knoll behind that was a caravan park with mobile homes of all shapes and sizes dotted across green lawns. There were tents too. Some were small, while others looked almost like houses.

'Granny says the caravan park has the best spot in town,' Freddy explained as they walked along the seawall that separated the harbour and the beach.

'Can we stay in a caravan one day, Mummy?' Clementine asked. She liked the thought of a little home where everything was in reach. It would be different to Penberthy House, which was enormous.

'That's a lovely idea, sweetheart,' Lady Clarissa said with a smile. 'Perhaps we can save that for a holiday for the two of us. I don't think Aunt Violet would approve.'

Clementine giggled at the thought of her great-aunt sleeping in a caravan, or even worse, a tent. 'Can we walk on the sand?'

Lady Clarissa nodded. 'Yes, of course. Give me your shoes and you and Freddy can take Lavender for a run along the water's edge.'

Clementine kicked off her sandals and Freddy did too. She carried Lavender down a set of old concrete steps and then set the pig down on the beach. Clementine and Freddy laughed as Lavender hopped about, unaccustomed to the strange texture under her trotters. Clarissa snapped some photographs of the unsuspecting children.

'She's a rabbit pig,' Freddy said as Lavender leapt into the air, her curly tail wriggling madly.

Clementine unclipped her lead and began to run towards the sea. The water was almost flat, with just the tiniest of waves curling onto the shore. The little pig chased after her but stopped when she reached the wet sand.

Lavender put one foot forward, dipping her trotter into a puddle, then she squealed and raced away towards Freddy.

Clarissa laughed and sat down on the steps, enjoying the warm sun on her back.

Eventually Clementine coaxed Lavender into the shallows. She and Freddy hooted with laughter as they ran in and out with Lavender chasing them.

After a while, Clementine took Lavender up onto the dry sand and the two of them plonked down. Freddy sat beside them.

'What class are you in?' Clementine asked the boy.

'Year Two,' Freddy replied.

'I'm in kindy,' Clementine said. 'I love school.'

'School's okay.' Freddy shrugged. 'But I like holidays better.'

Clementine stroked Lavender's tummy and the little pig grunted.

'Where are your mum and dad?' she asked, looking up at the sandy-haired boy.

'Dad had a conference and Mum went too, so that's why we're staying with Granny. Where's your dad?' Freddy asked.

Clementine paused. She remembered when she told Angus Archibald that her father was a mystery and he'd told her that was stupid.

'I don't know,' she replied. 'I've never met him.'

'You have a nice mum,' Freddy said, smiling. 'And your Uncle Digby is funny . . . but I'm not sure about that old lady.'

Clementine giggled. 'You mean Aunt Violet? She looks scarier than she is.'

'Do you want me to show you the rock pools?' Freddy asked.

Clementine nodded. Lavender was lying down with her eyes almost closed. Lady Clarissa wandered down onto the beach.

'Mummy, can we go to the rock pools, please?' Clementine asked.

'Yes, of course. I'll come too. Make sure you put your sandals on first. Those rocks can be sharp,' Lady Clarissa replied.

The children put their shoes back on, and raced towards the far end of the beach. A sheer cliff rose up from the rocks. With the harbour wall at one end and the cliff at the other, the beach was a perfect crescent. Lady Clarissa and Lavender followed behind. Lavender was busy investigating the sand, snout down.

'Look at this,' Freddy called as he jumped across a puddle onto the start of the rocky outcrop. He crouched down and stared into the clear pool.

'What is it?' Clementine squatted down beside him.

'Hang on.' Freddy scampered away then returned with a thin piece of driftwood. He poked it into the water.

A tentacle reached out and wrapped around the stick.

'It's an octopus!' Clementine gasped. She'd never seen one in real life.

'Isn't it cool?' Freddy said as the creature played tug of war with him. After a few seconds, the octopus released the stick and hid beneath a rock in the pool.

'What else is there?' Clementine asked eagerly.

Freddy leapt over another puddle towards a much bigger pool.

'Look at this!' he shouted as Clementine picked her way carefully over to join him.

A tiny crab scurried sideways, then was joined by several more. Clementine stared into the water, watching a large crab that was moving slowly along the bottom of the pool.

After a minute, she glanced up and noticed the way the rock shelf jutted out towards the sea. 'What's on the other side?' Clementine asked.

'There's another beach and something really amazing,' said Freddy.

'Mummy, can we go around further?' Clementine called to Lady Clarissa, who was now sitting on a large rock with Lavender beside her.

Lady Clarissa's voice carried back to them on the wind. 'Yes, darling, just be careful.'

Freddy led the way.

'This is a proper adventure,' said Clementine with a smile.

The children jumped and hopped their way across the uneven surface, careful not to slip into the pools. Around the point, the rock shelf curved back towards the cliffs. A few steps below them was a narrow inlet, and on the other side another tiny beach, with a patch of green grass behind it.

'Can you see anything?' Freddy asked, as he pointed at the cliff face on the other side of the inlet.

Clementine looked at the vines that tumbled over the top of the ledge and hung down like a veil.

'What is it?' she said, squinting.

Freddy pointed again. 'Just there.'

Clementine gasped. Hidden behind the vines was the outline of an opening. 'It's a cave!'

Freddy grinned.

'Have you been in there?' Clementine asked.

'Yes,' the boy nodded.

'But it's dark and we haven't got a torch,' Clementine said.

'I've got a special torch,' Freddy said, 'but it's at home.'

The boy made his way down the rocks, then jumped across the shallow inlet to the cave opening. He pulled the vines to one side. Clementine stayed back.

'We could bring your torch and look in there tomorrow,' Clementine suggested.

Freddy grinned at her. 'That's the best idea. It's not that scary but it will be better with a torch.'

He was trying to sound brave. When Freddy and Della had discovered the cave on their last visit to Endersley-on-Sea, Della had called him a sook because he hadn't wanted to go in. She'd pushed him through the vines and the darkness had covered him like a blanket. But he was sure it would be okay with a torch.

'We'll come back tomorrow,' said Freddy. He turned and jumped back across the narrow inlet and over the rocks to Clementine. The two children scurried back towards the main beach. They'd just rounded the headland when a voice screeched above the sound of the waves.

'Freddy! You have to come home. NOW!'

Freddy and Clementine reached Clarissa, who was looking towards the village end of the beach and the source of the noise.

The boy caught his breath and Clementine noticed he was jiggling nervously, as if he needed to go to the toilet. Della was standing at the top of the stairs with her hands on her hips. Her hair was blowing in the breeze and she looked a bit like a lion – only twice as fierce.

'It sounds like someone is looking for you, Freddy,' said Lady Clarissa. She squinted at Della in the distance.

'She can wait,' Freddy said, his voice wavering.

Clarissa was not so sure about that. She turned her attention back to Freddy and Clementine.

'Did you find anything interesting?' she asked.

Clementine and Freddy nodded.

'We saw an octopus,' Clementine said excitedly. 'And a cave. Didn't we, Freddy?'

The shouting was getting louder. Freddy looked past Lady Clarissa at his sister, who was now running along the beach towards them. He said nothing.

'Are you all right?' Clementine asked.

'I-I have to go,' Freddy said, and raced away towards Della.

'Thanks for the tour,' Clementine called after him. She watched as he reached his sister halfway along the beach. Clementine could just make out snatches of Della's words. She sounded angry. She grabbed the boy's shoulder and marched him away.

'I think Freddy's in trouble,' said Clementine. As she watched, Della pushed him hard in the middle of his back.

'Oh dear,' Lady Clarissa said. 'We'll have to make sure we ask Della to come tomorrow too.'

Clementine frowned. Freddy was lovely, but Della was something altogether different.

TIED UP

When Clementine and her mother returned to the house, Uncle Digby and Aunt Violet were in the front sitting room.

Uncle Digby looked up from the newspaper on his lap. 'Did you have a good walk?'

'We saw an octopus and some crabs and a cave!' Clementine enthused. 'But then Della came to get Freddy. So Mummy and I went for a walk around the harbour and I had an ice-cream and Lavender licked up the drips.'

'Look at that pig!' Aunt Violet shook her head at Lavender, who was encrusted with sand. 'You'll have to give her a rinse, Clementine.'

Rosamund Dent appeared in the doorway behind Clarissa. 'Oh, a bit of sand never hurt anyone,' she said with a smile. 'When you live by the sea you come to expect it. Now, would anyone like anything before I get started on dinner?'

Digby shook his head. 'No, thank you, Mrs Dent.'

'I wouldn't mind another cup of tea,' said Aunt Violet.

'You might turn into a cup of tea, the amount you drink,' Digby said pointedly.

'Well, you could get it for me,' Aunt Violet snapped, 'and save Mrs Dent the trouble.'

'Oh, it's no trouble. You're on holidays,' Mrs Dent smiled.

Digby hoisted himself to his feet. 'I'll come and give you a hand.'

Aunt Violet studied Mrs Dent and wondered how the woman's face could look like a sunbeam even when she wasn't smiling.

'I think we'll give Lavender a quick rinse in the shower. Clementine, you might like to have a bath too. Then you can be ready for bed straight after supper,' Clarissa suggested.

'But Mummy, we're on holidays,' Clementine said. 'Can I stay up later?'

'Of course, darling. I just thought you might like to feel a bit less salty,' her mother said.

'Dinner will be ready in about an hour,' said Mrs Dent, 'so you've got plenty of time. If you don't mind helping with the tea, Mr Pertwhistle, I might try to get those two of mine through the bath as well.'

'Certainly. And please call me Digby.'

'In that case, you must call me Rosamund,' Mrs Dent replied.

'And you can call me nauseated,' Violet Appleby muttered.

'I'm sorry Miss Appleby, did you say something?' Mrs Dent asked.

The old woman pursed her lips. 'No, I'm just a little parched.'

Clarissa stared at her aunt. She'd heard her perfectly.

Clementine scooped Lavender into her arms and followed her mother upstairs. There was no sign of Freddy or his sister anywhere. She wondered if their bedrooms were at the back of the house or above them, on the second floor. Wherever they were, they were awfully quiet.

Clementine took her bath while her mother gave Lavender a quick rinse in the shower. The little pig enjoyed the warm water, snapping at the spray and dancing about on the tiles. Clementine got dressed and wrapped Lavender in a towel.

'You smell nice,' Clementine said and nuzzled the pig's face. Lavender repaid her with a nibble on the nose.

'Clemmie, I'm going to get changed for dinner,' said her mother. 'Why don't you see if Freddy and Della want to play?'

Clementine took Lavender and headed down the hall. She didn't notice Della sitting near the top of the stairs leading up to the second floor.

'Why do you have a pig?' the child asked tartly.

Clementine spun around. 'Oh hello,' she said.

'Well?' Della stood up and stumped down the stairs towards Clementine. 'Why don't you have a normal pet like a dog or a cat or a guinea pig?'

'Mummy won her at the fair,' Clementine replied. Lavender looked up at her mistress and gave a squeak. 'Aunt Violet has a cat. His name is Pharaoh and he's a sphynx.'

'No, he's not. The Sphinx is a half-lion, half-man statue in Egypt. It's not a cat,' Della said.

'Yes, he is. He's bald and wrinkly and sometimes he scares the guests at home,' Clementine replied. 'I didn't know what he was at first because he doesn't look like any other cats I know.'

'Well, I have a pet python,' the girl said, her eyes narrowing. 'It's five metres long and we feed it all sorts of meaty little creatures.'

Clementine gulped. 'What's its name?'

Della hesitated for a moment. 'It's . . . it's Polly, if you must know.'

'That's a good name for a python,' Clemmie said quietly.

'Aren't you scared?' Della demanded.

Clementine drew herself up tall and shook her head. 'No, I'm sure that your granny doesn't let her roam around the house. I have a toy python. Once, I left it in the Rose Room and the lady who was staying there screamed and screamed because she thought it was real. It wasn't very good for business because Mummy had to give her a big discount and make her lots of tea so she would calm down.'

Della looked confused.

'We live in a hotel,' added Clementine.

'No, you don't,' the girl said.

Clementine nodded. 'Yes, we do. It's called Penberthy House and it's very big and old and it's getting a new roof, so that's why we've come on holidays.'

'Well, it's not as big as our hotel,' Della snapped.

Clementine looked around her. Penberthy House was much larger and grander than Mrs Dent's guesthouse.

Della glared at her.

'I'm going downstairs now,' Clementine said.

'Why?' Della snapped.

'Because Mummy said I should find Freddy so we can play a game,' Clementine said.

'Do you always do what your mother tells you?' Della asked.

Clementine thought about it and then nodded. 'I try to.'

'You're such a baby. Only babies do every-thing their mothers tell them,' Della sneered. 'Anyway, Freddy's tied up at the moment.'

Clementine frowned. 'Oh.'

'You can play a game with me instead,' Della said.

Clementine looked at the girl. 'But I thought you only played with people who were over seven.'

'Usually I do. But seeing that there's no one over seven here to play with now, I suppose you'll have to do.'

'You don't have to,' Clementine said.

'Don't you *want* to play with me now?' Della sighed.

'Okay,' Clementine nodded. 'What should we play?'

'Hide-and-seek,' Della said. 'You hide and I'll find you and the pig.'

Clementine smiled. She liked hide-and-seek – especially at home where there were lots of places to disappear. But she had no idea where to hide here. She'd only been downstairs and in her own room with her mother.

'I don't know where to go,' Clementine said.

'Up there.' Della pointed to the top floor. 'But you have to stay on the left-hand side of the stairs.'

Clementine gulped.

'You do know your left and right, don't you?' asked Della.

Clementine nodded. Secretly, she was trying to remember which was which.

'Can Freddy play too?' Clementine asked.

'No. He went to the beach without me, so now I'm playing a game without him,' Della said, flicking her fingernails. 'Well, off you go. I'll count to fifty and then I'm coming to get you.'

Clementine picked up Lavender and scampered up the stairs to the top floor. She reached the landing and looked each way. She couldn't remember if left was this way or that way. There were several doors along both sides of the corridor. Clementine ran to the one furthest along. She pushed it open.

Inside was a pretty room with blue floral wallpaper. There was a large bookshelf and an iron bedstead. Clementine wondered if this was where Della slept. There was another door on the far wall. Clementine turned the handle and found herself in a bathroom. She hid behind the towel hanging on the rail, pulling it down so it skimmed the floor.

Clementine heard a voice in the hallway.

'Ready or not, here I come,' Della shouted. But the footsteps seemed to be running away.

Clementine thought about left and right. Mrs Bottomley had taught the class that the left hand makes the shape of a capital L. Clementine put Lavender down and held up her hands. Oops – she'd turned right at the top of the stairs.

'Come on, Lavender, let's go before we get in trouble.' Clementine picked up the little pig and they dashed out of the bathroom and back through the bedroom. She opened the door and peeked out. Della was nowhere to be seen. Clementine scurried along the hall back to the landing and crouched down beside a fire extinguisher, with Lavender sitting next to her.

'Where are you?' Della called in a singsong voice.

Clementine held her breath. She could feel her heart beating in her ears. The door furthest down the corridor to the left banged and Della stomped outside. Clementine was sure that the girl would spot her but instead she dived through the next door.

'I'm going to find you,' Della cried.

Clementine became aware of a tapping noise.

'What's that?' she whispered and looked at Lavender with a frown. The noise was getting louder. There was a mumbly voice as well as the tapping now.

Della reappeared in the hallway, banging the door shut behind her.

'You'd better not be down the other end or you'll be in trouble, Clementine! I told you not to go there!' Della was stomping towards the child and her pig.

Clementine crouched down as far as she could go and Della walked right past her. Lavender let out a little grunt and the child spun around.

'There you are!' Della pointed her finger. 'How come I didn't see you before?'

Clementine shrugged. 'I'm good at hiding. What's that tapping noise?'

Della listened. 'It's Polly. She wants her dinner.'

Clementine's eyes grew wide. 'I have to go downstairs. I think Mummy's calling me.' She picked up Lavender and scurried away.

'But it's my turn to hide,' Della protested. She pouted and stamped her foot.

Clementine raced down two flights of stairs and along the hall to the kitchen. She pushed her way inside and let out a deep breath.

'Are you all right, dear?' Mrs Dent turned from where she was stirring a huge pot on a gigantic old stove.

Clementine nodded.

Digby Pertwhistle was busy doing a crossword, Lady Clarissa was flicking through one of Mrs Dent's cookbooks and Aunt Violet was sitting at the other end of the table, nibbling a biscuit and drinking tea.

'Would you like a glass of milk and a brownie?' Mrs Dent asked.

Uncle Digby looked up and grinned. 'They're delicious, Clementine.'

'Do you think that's wise, Clemmie? Dinner's almost ready,' her mother asked.

'I'm really hungry.' Clementine climbed onto the chair beside Uncle Digby. Lavender snuffled about the kitchen floor looking for crumbs. 'And I promise to eat all my dinner.'

Clarissa smiled. 'All right. We are on holidays, after all. An extra treat won't hurt.'

'What have you been up to?' Uncle Digby asked.

'I was playing hide-and-seek with Della,' Clementine said.

Her mother smiled. 'Oh, that's good, darling.'

Clementine turned to Mrs Dent. 'Does Polly live upstairs?'

'Polly?' Mrs Dent frowned as she poured Clementine's milk.

'Della said that she has a python called Polly,' Clementine explained.

'Della has a good imagination, that's what she has.' Mrs Dent rolled her eyes, wondering what sort of dreadful tales her granddaughter had been filling Clementine's head with.

'I heard something banging and Della said it was Polly,' Clementine said.

Mrs Dent placed the milk and a plump brownie in front of Clementine.

'No, no, there's no Polly,' Mrs Dent said, shaking her head. 'You don't need to worry about that.'

Clementine sighed. 'Phew. When Aunt Violet first brought Pharaoh to our house I thought he was a snake and I was really worried that he might want to eat Lavender for dinner.'

'Pharaoh loves that pig,' said Aunt Violet, looking up from the book she was reading. 'Oh, I wonder how my baby's getting on.'

'I'm sure Mrs Mogg's spoiling him rotten and he's having a wonderful time,' said Lady Clarissa.

'Clementine, was Freddy playing with you too?' asked Mrs Dent. She opened the oven to check on the roast inside.

The child shook her head. 'No. Della said that he was tied up.'

'Oh no, not again!' Mrs Dent slammed the oven door. 'Poor boy. I'll be back in a minute. Digby, can you watch the stove, please?'

In a flash Mrs Dent was gone.

MEMORIES

Mrs Dent returned to the kitchen a short while later with Freddy and Della in tow. The girl's eyes were red-rimmed and her cheeks were puffy.

Mrs Dent headed for the stove to take over from Uncle Digby. Della walked straight to the biscuit barrel and removed the lid.

'No, Della,' her grandmother said without turning her attention from the stove. 'You and your brother can set the table in the dining room, please.'

'I'll help the youngsters,' said Uncle Digby.

The old woman smiled at him. 'Thank you, Digby. I'm a bit behind, I'm afraid.'

'I thought you were on holidays, Uncle Digby,' Clementine said.

'I am. But Mrs Dent has a lot to do and you know I can't sit still for long,' he replied.

'That's true,' Clementine said. 'Uncle Digby's always busy at home. He polishes the silver a lot.'

Lady Clarissa asked if she could help their host with anything else. Mrs Dent insisted she was fine and suggested the ladies make themselves comfortable in the sitting room until dinner was ready. Clementine gathered up Lavender, who had found herself a warm spot beside the oven. She followed her mother and Aunt Violet down the hall and into the front room. Aunt Violet went back to her book and Lady Clarissa flicked through a magazine.

Board games, colouring pencils and sheets of paper were stacked on a bookshelf in the corner. Clementine decided to draw the rock pools and the octopus she and Freddy had found earlier.

A little while later, Freddy appeared at the door and announced that dinner was ready in the dining room.

Clementine skipped towards the boy, holding her picture.

'Do you like it?' she asked.

Freddy nodded. 'That's cool. I love octopuses.'

The children scooted down to the dining room and took their seats. The tension from earlier had evaporated and everyone was enjoying the delicious roast lamb and vegetables.

This time Clementine was sitting between her mother and Freddy, and Della was at the other end of the table next to her grandmother.

'So, children, where do you live?' Uncle Digby asked.

'In Parsley Vale,' Freddy said.

'Our father is the boss of the whole town,' Della said smugly.

Aunt Violet looked up and arched her left eyebrow. 'Oh, really. What does he do?'

'He's hardly that, Della. You must stop exaggerating,' her grandmother tutted.

Della wrinkled her nose.

'He's the Inspector Chief of the police,' said Freddy.

'No, he's not,' Della snapped. He's the Chief Inspector. Anyway, I got to ride in the police car really fast with the siren on.'

'Well, that sounds dangerous,' Uncle Digby said.

Della nodded. 'It was. We were chasing after a bank robber.'

Aunt Violet and Lady Clarissa exchanged frowns.

'You weren't even there,' Freddy said.

'Yes, I was,' Della spat. 'You don't know anything.'

'Della, perhaps you should stop telling stories and eat your dinner,' suggested Mrs Dent.

Della poked her tongue out at Freddy and made a face at Clementine.

There was a squeak and a grunt and Lavender waddled into the room.

72

'Oh, you really are the most precious creature,' said Mrs Dent as the little pig sniffed her way around the table. 'Do you have any other pets, Clementine?'

The child shook her head. 'Aunt Violet has Pharaoh. He's a sphynx.'

'Why didn't you bring him too?' Mrs Dent asked.

'Pharaoh is something of a Houdini,' said Aunt Violet.

'Oh, an escape artist,' Mrs Dent said, smiling.

Clementine nodded. 'Hopefully he doesn't escape from Mrs Mogg's house.'

'Oh, Clementine, please don't even say such a thing. I don't know what I'd do if anything happened to my darling boy.' Aunt Violet brushed a hand over her eyes.

'It's just a stupid cat,' Della said.

Aunt Violet stared at the girl in horror. 'How dare you? Pharaoh is anything but a stupid cat. He's intelligent and he's sweet and . . .'

'He's ugly but, you know, I've got used to him now. He's really quite lovely,' Clementine added.

Aunt Violet glared at Clementine. Her mother and Uncle Digby tried hard not to smile. If there was one thing they could always rely on, it was Clementine's honesty.

'Goodness,' Mrs Dent laughed. 'You just reminded me of another funny pet, Clementine. When I was a little girl my cousin Teddy had a –'

'Salamander,' Digby Pertwhistle finished the woman's sentence.

Mrs Dent looked surprised. 'That's exactly right.'

'How did you know that, Uncle Digby?' Clementine asked.

The man grinned. 'Rosamund, were you by any chance called Mozzie as a girl?'

A huge smile spread across the woman's face, as if that one word had opened a vault of memories. 'Oh, my goodness. I've got it. You're Diggy,' she said and began to laugh.

Aunt Violet rolled her eyes. 'Diggy and Mozzie, good gracious.'

'But how do you know each other?' Clementine asked.

Mrs Dent took a sip of water and then began the story. 'We were just children. I was about eight or nine.'

'And I would have been twelve,' Uncle Digby added.

'Your Uncle Digby came to stay with my cousin Teddy, here in this house. It was my aunt and uncle's holiday home. They were much better off than we were and my parents were always happy for me to stay with the "posh relatives", as they called them.'

'Teddy and I teased little Mozzie constantly,' Digby Pertwhistle said.

'And I adored the pair of them.' Mrs Dent smiled. 'I was like a puppy following them around everywhere.'

'Has anything changed?' Aunt Violet mumbled to herself.

'Why didn't you see each other again after that?' Clementine asked.

Uncle Digby began to explain. 'Teddy went off to boarding school. I don't know why we lost touch. My parents used to bring me to

Endersley-on-Sea every summer but Teddy was never here.'

'My uncle took a job overseas so the house was hardly ever used, as I recall. Teddy and his sisters spent their holidays in Greece after that. Gosh, I adored Teddy and Diggy. I used to spy on the pair of you when you played cards. Diggy was a very handsome lad.'

Uncle Digby's cheeks flushed. 'Oh, get off with you. My ears stuck out far too much and I was as tall and skinny as a string bean.'

'You could get married,' Clementine said. 'Uncle Digby never had a wife and your husband died, so you could.'

'Clementine, what ridiculous twaddle are you talking about now?' Aunt Violet snapped. 'As if Mrs Dent would want to marry Pertwhistle. He's hardly a catch, is he?'

But Rosamund Dent had a twinkle in her eye. 'I don't know, Miss Appleby. I'd say any woman would be lucky to have him. I'm surprised you haven't snapped him up.'

Aunt Violet shuddered.

'Aunt Violet doesn't need another husband. She's already had three,' Clementine said.

'Clementine! I'll thank you to keep my personal business private,' Aunt Violet huffed.

Digby stood up and began to clear the plates.

'Thank you, *Diggy*. I'll organise dessert,' Mrs Dent said.

'What is it?' Della asked.

'Lemon meringue pie and ice-cream,' said Mrs Dent.

'You said we could have chocolate pudding,' Della whined.

'And I think you could have an early bed time,' Aunt Violet said sternly.

TO THE BEACH

A sliver of sunlight shone through the small gap in the curtains in the front bedroom. Clementine yawned and stretched her arms above her head. She'd dreamt about building a sandcastle and couldn't wait to get to the beach. She was looking forward to testing out the pretty red polka-dot swimming costume Mrs Mogg had made her, too. The kind woman had even sewn a matching hat for Lavender. Aunt Violet had said there was no way she was going to the beach with a pig in a bonnet.

'Hello sleepyhead,' said Lady Clarissa. She put her book on the side table and pushed back the bedcovers.

Clementine rolled over on her own single bed, which was beside her mother's, and blinked her eyes awake. 'Hello Mummy.'

'Did you sleep well, darling?'

Clementine nodded. 'I was tired.'

'Well, you and Freddy did stay up quite late playing cards,' her mother reminded her.

Lady Clarissa and Clementine put on their swimming costumes. Clarissa popped a yellow sundress over the top and Clementine had a matching polka dot dress to put on over her bathers. Clementine picked up Lavender's red lead and the happy trio set off downstairs for breakfast.

'Goodness me, I thought you two were going to sleep the day away,' Aunt Violet said as she set her teacup down with a light thud.

Uncle Digby looked up from his newspaper, pulled a face at Violet and smiled hello to Clarissa and Clementine.

'I suppose that's why it's called a holiday, Aunt Violet,' Clarissa said. 'I haven't slept in for years.'

Clementine thought it was strange for Aunt Violet to talk about sleeping in. At home she did it all the time.

'We're going to the beach,' the child announced. 'Are you coming too?'

'Yes, I think I might,' Aunt Violet replied.

Clementine clapped her hands in delight. 'Will you come swimming?'

'Clementine, I haven't been swimming in the sea since I was a teenager. I'm not about to start again now.'

The child's face dropped.

'Oh, don't look like that. I might wade in the shallows but that's all,' the old woman said.

'I like your dress,' said Clementine, admiring Aunt Violet's aqua-blue kaftan.

'Yes, I haven't had a chance to wear it since the cruise,' Aunt Violet replied. She was referring to her three-month trip aboard the *Queen Mary 2*. Lady Clarissa had won the holiday in a competition and kindly given it to her aunt.

'Where's Mrs Dent?' Clementine asked.

'She's gone to get the children up,' said Uncle Digby.

'Are you coming to the beach too, Uncle Digby?' Clementine asked.

The old man nodded.

'Will *you* take me swimming?' she begged.

'Sweetheart, I'll take you,' her mother said. 'Please stop badgering Aunt Violet and Uncle Digby. Remember, they're on holidays too and they can do whatever they like.'

'You know what, Clementine. I used to love bodysurfing on this beach. I might just dig out my swimming trunks and join you,' Digby said with a grin.

Aunt Violet's face contorted.

'Is something the matter, Aunt Violet?' said Clementine.

'I don't need to see a great tall prune on the beach. Prunes belong at the breakfast table.'

'Who are you calling a prune?' Digby Pertwhistle asked.

'You, you silly old fool,' Aunt Violet scoffed.

'I'll have you know there are quite a few muscles under this shirt.' Uncle Digby raised his left arm and flexed his biceps.

Clementine giggled. 'Uncle Digby, you don't have any muscles –'

'Thank you, Clementine. I thought you'd be sticking up for me.' The old man grinned.

'– but Aunt Violet has more wrinkles than you.' The rest of the sentence was out of her mouth before she had time to stop it.

'I do not,' Aunt Violet retorted. 'Pertwhistle's got wrinkles on his wrinkles.'

The kitchen door flew open and Freddy rushed into the room. He was followed by his sister, who seemed to be dragging her feet. Freddy sat down next to Clementine, but Della stalked to the other end of the table and ignored everyone completely.

Mrs Dent entered next, her face shining. 'Good morning, Clarissa and Clementine.'

Lavender squeaked.

'And you too, Lavender.'

'Hello Mrs Dent,' Clementine and her mother said in unison.

'It's a beautiful day,' the woman declared, 'but I believe we could be in for a storm this afternoon.'

'Are you taking us to the beach too, Granny?' Freddy asked.

'No, darling. I'm sorry, but I have a lot to do this morning.'

'But you always have a lot to do,' the boy moaned.

Clementine looked at him and smiled. 'You can come with us.'

Clementine and Freddy had been talking about exploring the cave before they went to bed last night.

'Yes, of course he can. And Della too,' said Lady Clarissa.

On hearing her name, the girl glanced up at Clementine. Clementine's tummy twinged again, just as it had the day before.

'Oh, Clarissa, are you sure?' Mrs Dent asked.

'Yes, of course. Uncle Digby and Aunt Violet are coming along so there'll be plenty of eyes to keep watch.'

'Would you like to go?' Mrs Dent asked her grandchildren.

The boy nodded furiously.

Della shrugged. 'I suppose so.'

Freddy beamed at Clementine. 'I'll get my bucket and spade,' he said, then leaned over and whispered to Clementine, 'and my torch.'

'We can make a sandcastle,' Clementine said. 'I'll take my bucket and spade too.'

Breakfast was over quickly. Mrs Dent insisted on packing some freshly baked chocolate cake and honey jumbles, along with the leftover brownies and some apples and bananas. She added a thermos of tea and some cold drinks too.

Uncle Digby retrieved the cooler bag, umbrella and jazzy blue beach chairs that had been Lady Clarissa's most recent competition win.

Della and Freddy reappeared with their swimmers on underneath their clothes. Freddy's face was lathered white with sunscreen.

Mrs Dent took her grandchildren to one side. 'Now, you make sure that you do everything you're asked, please. I don't want to hear any reports of bad behaviour. And have you put on sunscreen, Della?'

'Yes,' the child grouched. 'I don't get sunburnt, anyway.'

Mrs Dent gave her granddaughter a sceptical look, then turned to Lady Clarissa.

'Thank you, Clarissa. I do appreciate having some time to catch up on the paperwork,' the old woman said.

'It's a pleasure. Believe me, I know how hard it is to get all the jobs done when you have a house full of guests,' Lady Clarissa replied.

Aunt Violet had disappeared upstairs and returned wearing the most enormous blue sunhat.

'Good heavens,' Uncle Digby gasped. 'Do you

realise there's a flying saucer on your head, Miss Appleby?'

Clementine laughed out loud.

'You know absolutely nothing about fashion, do you, Pertwhistle?' The old woman rolled her eyes behind her dark glasses.

'Uncle Digby, I think Aunt Violet looks beautiful,' Clementine said admiringly.

'As long as she doesn't injure anyone on the street, I suppose,' Uncle Digby teased. 'She could take someone's head off with that thing.'

'And what are you wearing?' Aunt Violet looked the old man up and down. 'I doubt those twig legs of yours have seen the sun since you were a boy.'

Clementine had never seen Uncle Digby in shorts before either. His legs *were* a bit like a seagull's, she decided.

'That's it. I'm calling a truce. It's about time you two tried to be nice to one another,' Lady Clarissa said sternly.

Uncle Digby hung his head. 'Oh, all right. I'll do my best.'

'If I must,' Aunt Violet agreed.

Clementine and her mother looked at each other and smiled.

'I think we should be off,' said Lady Clarissa. She bustled about taking charge of her motley crew.

Clementine and Freddy walked ahead with Lavender, and Aunt Violet and Uncle Digby came behind.

'So tell me, Della, are you having a lovely holiday?' Lady Clarissa asked as she closed the garden gate behind her. 'It must be nice to spend time with your granny.'

'Not really,' the child replied. 'Granny's bossy and boring.'

'Oh,' Clarissa mouthed. It seemed that Della might be a little harder to thaw than she'd thought.

NEW FRIENDS

The beach was dotted with families staking out their spots, but there was still lots of space. Aunt Violet led the way down the sand. She found a patch far enough from the water that she wouldn't have to worry about any splashes.

Uncle Digby pitched the new blue beach umbrella while the others rolled out their towels and unfolded the three low beach chairs. Aunt Violet lowered herself onto her chair and immediately pulled a fashion magazine from her oversized beach bag.

Della plonked herself onto the sand beside her brother and proceeded to lecture him. 'We're going to build a mermaid's castle and I'm going to be the mermaid princess.'

'But I don't want to do that,' Freddy said. 'I don't even know what a mermaid's castle looks like.'

Freddy and Clementine were eager to go back to the rock pools and have a proper look in the cave, but Freddy didn't want Della to come. She would just take over, as always.

'We should do what she says and then we can go and look at the cave later,' Clementine whispered to Freddy.

The boy nodded. 'We want to build a proper castle,' he told his sister.

'No, it's a mermaid's castle. I'm in charge because I'm the oldest,' the girl insisted. 'I'll tell you what to do.'

Lady Clarissa cleared her throat. 'Darling, have you put sunscreen on Lavender yet?' The sun already had a bite to it.

Clementine nodded. Lavender was sitting on the towel beside her.

'Sunscreen? On a pig?' Della scoffed.

'Lavender gets sunburnt more easily than you and me,' Clementine explained. 'That's why pigs roll in mud – to protect their skin. Lavender doesn't like mud very much, so we have to put sunscreen on her.'

'That's stupid,' Della said. 'Pigs aren't proper pets, anyway.'

Freddy ignored his sister and grinned at Clementine. 'Does Lavender have a sunhat?'

She nodded and rushed over to pull it from her mother's beach bag.

'That's ridiculous,' Della snorted as Clementine put the little bonnet on Lavender's head.

'I think she looks cute,' Freddy said.

Della ignored her brother and stood up. 'Come on then, you'd better get the buckets and spades and start building my mermaid's castle.'

Clementine and Freddy did as they were told.

'We're building it right there.' Della pointed at a spot a little closer to the water. 'Now, this is what it has to look like. I want a proper castle with towers and turrets and then there has to be a mermaid's tail next to it and when it's finished I'll be the body and you have to dig underneath so my legs are covered by the tail . . .'

The girl's voice droned on and on. Freddy thought it sounded very complicated.

'Mummy, can you look after Lavender?' Clementine asked.

'Of course, darling.' Lady Clarissa took the little pig's lead and lashed it to her beach chair.

Lavender squealed as Clementine rushed off to catch up with Freddy.

'When you want to go for a swim, come and let me know,' Lady Clarissa called after Clementine. 'And don't wander off.'

Della stood with her hands on her hips and ordered Freddy to start digging. She directed Clementine to fill the buckets with water so they could shape the sand. Clemmie ran to the surf's edge and back several times while Della stood like a policeman directing traffic.

As the mermaid's tail took shape, Clementine's and Freddy's faces grew red and beads of sweat trickled down their temples.

'It doesn't look right,' Della whined. 'You need to make a scaly pattern.'

'Maybe you could find some shells to decorate the tail?' Clementine suggested.

'I *already* thought of that,' Della said, rolling her eyes. But she raced down the beach all the same.

'Your sister's bossy,' Clementine said.

Freddy nodded. 'She'd be even worse if you weren't here.'

Clementine wondered how much more horrible the girl could be. She felt very sorry for Freddy.

The two children were busy working on their construction and didn't see a group of girls approaching.

'That looks amazing,' gasped one girl. She

had cascading chocolate curls and brown eyes as big as saucers.

Clementine looked up and shielded her eyes from the sun. 'Thank you,' she said.

'Do you want some help?' asked another girl. She had red hair and freckles, and wore a white sunhat.

Freddy nodded. 'Yes, please.'

'My name's Alice-Miranda Highton-Smith-Kennington-Jones,' the brown-haired girl said. 'This is Millie.' She pointed at the red-haired girl. 'And that's Jacinta.' She pointed at a taller blonde-haired girl.

Millie and Jacinta both said hello.

'What are your names?' Jacinta asked.

'I'm Clementine Rose.'

'And I'm Freddy,' the boy answered.

'Are you brother and sister?' Alice-Miranda asked.

Freddy smiled.

Clementine did too. 'No, we just met yester-day,' she said.

'You look like twins,' said Jacinta.

'We're having a holiday in Millie's caravan, just up there,' Alice-Miranda said.

'I'd like to stay in a caravan but I don't think Aunt Violet would like it,' said Clementine.

'Who's Aunt Violet?' Millie asked.

'She's my grandpa's sister and she's very old and Mummy once said that she was crusty like a barnacle,' Clementine explained.

The three girls giggled, imagining an old lady covered in little shells.

'Do you want to help build the tower?' Freddy asked.

Alice-Miranda nodded. The girls pitched in and soon they had a very impressive castle next to the mermaid's tail.

'Do you live far away?' Alice-Miranda asked the children.

'In Parsley Vale,' Freddy said.

Clementine nodded. 'I live in Penberthy Floss.'

'Really?' said Alice-Miranda. 'That's just next to the village I live in, Highton Mill. And Parsley Vale is close to our boarding school too.'

'I go to Ellery Prep,' Clementine said.

'What a lovely coincidence. I went there too and my friend Poppy goes there now. She and her brother and mummy and daddy live on our farm,' Alice-Miranda explained.

'Really?' Clementine said excitedly. 'Poppy's my friend too!'

'You'll have to come and visit her in the holidays. I could take you riding on my pony, Bonaparte,' Alice-Miranda offered.

Clementine nodded. She'd never been on a horse before but she was keen to try.

Lady Clarissa untied Lavender's lead and walked the little pig towards the group of children. 'Hello,' she said, smiling at the girls and Freddy. 'I see you're making friends.'

Alice-Miranda introduced herself and the other girls to Lady Clarissa.

'Is that a teacup pig?' Millie's eyes were almost popping out of her head.

'Yes. Her name's Lavender,' Clementine said.

'She's adorable.' Millie scooped the little pig into her arms.

Lady Clarissa looked around and realised that Della was missing. 'Where's your sister, Freddy?'

He shrugged. Lady Clarissa scanned the beach.

'Della went to find some shells,' said Clementine.

Clarissa's heart pounded. She'd promised to keep a close eye on the children for Mrs Dent.

'Who's Della?' Alice-Miranda asked.

'She's my sister,' Freddy said.

'We can help you look for her,' said Alice-Miranda. 'Don't worry, I'm sure she can't have gone far.'

Lady Clarissa's eyes searched the crowd. She wasn't nearly as sure as Alice-Miranda.

BEASTLY CREATURES

Just as the group was about to set off, a piercing scream sliced the air. The beach-goers looked towards the noise and several people leapt to their feet.

A young lifeguard sprinted towards the water.

'Help!' a voice shouted.

'Oh no, that's Della!' Lady Clarissa spun around and raced towards the growing crowd of onlookers.

She pushed her way through the people, with Clementine and Freddy close behind her.

Alice-Miranda and Jacinta followed. Millie stayed back, holding onto Lavender.

'Della, what happened? Are you hurt?' Lady Clarissa looked at the child, whose face was the colour of a tomato.

The lifeguard was doing his best to calm the girl. 'Miss, did something sting you?' A swarm of jellyfish had been sighted further up the coast.

'It was in the water,' the child sobbed. 'It wrapped around my leg.'

The tall man directed the crowd of onlookers to stand back as he scanned the shallows. 'Was it a stinger or a jellyfish?' he asked. He couldn't see any marks on the girl.

'I don't know!' Della cried. She turned around to look at the surf. 'It could have been a shark. There it is!' She pointed.

'Seaweed?' the lifeguard asked, a bewildered look on his face. 'Is that all?'

'What do you mean?' Della yelled. 'It was beastly. It wrapped around my leg and pulled me out into the water and it made me drop all my shells and now I haven't got any for the mermaid's tail.'

Clementine noticed a pile of shells being tossed about as the water came in and was sucked back out again.

The young man frowned at Della and then turned to the crowd. 'All right, folks, everything's fine. There's nothing to see here.'

Freddy sighed. He turned and walked back up the sand.

'Della, why don't you come and have a drink and something to eat?' Lady Clarissa said kindly. She noticed the child's bright pink shoulders and face. 'Did you put any sunscreen on this morning?'

'Yes, of course I did. It just didn't work,' Della sniffed.

Clementine raced back to their mermaid castle and grabbed a bucket. She ran to the water's edge and tried to gather up as many of the shells as she could see.

Lady Clarissa guided Della up the beach. 'Come on, I think I'll take you home. That sunburn looks nasty.'

Tears were streaming down the child's face. 'My leg hurts,' Della sniffled. She wiped her nose with the back of her hand and reached down to scratch her thigh. 'Something did sting me. It wasn't just the seaweed.'

Lady Clarissa stopped and inspected Della's leg. 'I'm sure your grandmother will have some calamine lotion.'

Lady Clarissa turned and called back to Clementine, 'Clemmie, why don't you take your friends up to our umbrella. Tell Aunt Violet and Uncle Digby that I'm taking Della home and ask them to keep an eye on you and Freddy. You can all have some drinks and a snack.'

The child nodded. Her mother and Della walked away up the beach.

Clementine led her new friends to where Aunt Violet and Uncle Digby were sitting.

'Hello Aunt Violet,' Clementine shouted as she bounded up to her chair.

The woman gave a snort. 'Good heavens, Clementine, you don't need to scare me half to death.'

'Were you asleep?'

'Of course not.' Aunt Violet sat up straighter.

'Mummy said that we could have something to eat and a drink.' She motioned towards her friends.

'Are we taking in orphans?' Aunt Violet asked. She tapped her foot on Uncle Digby's bare leg. The man was snoring gently.

He grunted awake. 'Yes, yes, what is it?'

'We've got to feed the children. I don't know where Clarissa has swanned off to,' Aunt Violet grumbled.

'Mummy's taken Della home because she's got a sunburn,' Clementine said. 'And she asked if you could look after us.'

Aunt Violet grimaced. Uncle Digby dug around inside the cooler bag and handed drinks to the children.

'Hello, I'm Alice-Miranda Highton-Smith-Kennington-Jones,' one of the new girls said. She offered her hand to Aunt Violet.

The woman perked up immediately. 'Did you say Highton-Smith-Kennington-Jones?'

Alice-Miranda nodded.

'Oh, how lovely to meet you.' Aunt Violet took the child's tiny hand into hers and gave it a shake. 'We're practically neighbours, you know. We're at Penberthy House.'

Alice-Miranda smiled and introduced her friends.

Jacinta stepped forward to say hello and tripped on the edge of a towel. She went flying and sent sand all over Aunt Violet.

The woman's face contorted.

'I'm sorry,' Jacinta said meekly.

'So you should be,' Aunt Violet tutted.

The children enjoyed their snacks and then went back to the sandcastle. They decorated it happily until Millie's mother called the older girls to go in.

'We're leaving tomorrow morning,' Alice-Miranda explained. 'But I'm sure I'll see you again at home, Clementine.'

Clementine hoped so too. She and Freddy farewelled their new friends.

'Do you want to go and look at the cave now?' Freddy asked Clementine.

The girl nodded. 'But we'll have to take Uncle Digby or Aunt Violet.'

'Yes, but they can just have a rest where your mother did yesterday,' said Freddy. He didn't want the grown-ups spoiling their adventure.

Clementine returned a minute later with Uncle Digby in tow. 'You don't have to come all the way with us, Uncle Digby. There's a big rock you can sit on.'

'All right, then. Can I bring my book?' the old man asked.

Clementine nodded.

Uncle Digby walked back to their camp site to get it.

'Where's Lavender?' Freddy asked.

'She's asleep. Aunt Violet said that she'd look after her.'

Clementine and Freddy were armed with buckets in case they found any treasure to bring back, and Freddy had the little torch in the pocket of his board shorts.

Uncle Digby walked back to the children.

'Don't worry, Uncle Digby, we'll be very careful,' Clementine told the old man. She grabbed hold of Freddy's hand and they ran off towards the rocks.

A THRILLING DISCOVERY

F reddy and Clementine hopped over the rocks just as they had done the day before. The pools of water sparkled in the sun as Clementine crouched down to look for the octopus. It was doing a good job of hiding. She could only see some shells and a couple of tiny crabs.

'Come on, Clementine,' Freddy shouted as he jumped from rock to rock.

She caught up to him where the rock shelf curved around the small headland.

To get to the cave, they had to climb down to a lower level. Clementine noticed that the waves were bigger now and every few minutes the surf would spray upwards, sending a shower of sea water onto the edge of the platform. A little channel ran between the rocks and cave's mouth, but there was only a trickle of water in it.

Clementine and Freddy hopped down onto the sand.

'Do you really think there could be treasure inside?' Clementine asked, her eyes wide.

Freddy shrugged. 'I didn't find any last time, but I didn't have a torch then so I couldn't see properly. Granny says there used to be pirates on this coast a long time ago.'

Clementine's tummy fluttered. This really was a proper adventure.

Freddy took the torch out of his pocket. He pulled the vines back from the cave entrance and shone the light inside. Then he took Clementine's hand and the two children crept inside.

'It smells awful,' Clementine whispered.

Freddy held his nose. 'Yuck! Like dead fish.'

He shone the light straight ahead of them. Five rectangular stones stuck out of the sand like giant's teeth. Then he directed the torch at the sandy floor and up to the smooth curve of the roof. It didn't look like there was any treasure. Just a couple of empty soft-drink bottles lying in the sand. The cave wasn't nearly as deep as Freddy had hoped, either.

Clementine squeezed Freddy's hand. 'It's really smelly in here. Do you want to go back for a swim?'

He nodded.

Just as the children turned to leave, Freddy's torchlight caught something unexpected.

'Did you see that?' he asked.

'What?' Clementine whispered.

Freddy pointed the torch back to the same spot. Poking out from behind one of the stones were two red eyes. They glowed in the darkness.

'What's that?' the boy breathed.

'I don't know.' Clementine's heart was pounding.

All of a sudden there was a strange barking sound.

Freddy squinted. 'It must be a puppy.'

'What if it's lost?' Clementine said. 'We should help it.'

'Maybe I can keep it?' Freddy felt a rush of excitement as he imagined a new pet. He loved Lavender and had been planning to ask his parents if he could have a pet pig – but a dog might be even better.

'Here, boy,' Freddy said soothingly.

The two children walked closer to the creature. It had a long body and a funny oval head with tiny little ears sticking out at the sides.

'That's a strange-looking dog,' Clementine said.

The creature barked again and stretched upwards. It danced from one side to the other.

'That's not a dog,' Freddy gasped. 'It's a seal.'

Clementine didn't know much about seals, but this one was small and very cute. She walked closer and reached out.

'No!' Freddy said. 'He's a wild animal. You can't touch him.'

Clementine jumped back.

'We learned about seals at school,' Freddy said. 'If people pet them, they get confused.'

'What do they eat?' Clementine asked.

'Fish,' Freddy replied.

'Oh! That's why it's so stinky in here,' Clementine said. 'Do you think it's lost?'

'I don't know,' Freddy said with a shrug. 'There are lots of seals on the next beach around from here. He looks okay. Maybe he's just having some time out from a bossy sister.'

Clementine giggled. 'Do you think we should tell Uncle Digby?'

Freddy watched as the creature swayed from side to side.

'You know, he could be our special secret,' Freddy said. He liked the idea of having something only he and Clementine knew about.

Clementine nodded. 'Okay.'

The seal looked at the children with its big brown eyes.

'Come on, Freddy, we should go or Uncle Digby might get worried.' Clementine tugged at the boy's arm.

The two children left the cave and scrambled back up onto the higher rock ledge. They trod carefully between the pools.

Freddy's eyes were still shining with excitement. 'That was so cool!'

'I know,' Clementine said.

'Hello there,' said Uncle Digby as the children approached. 'I was just about to come and find you. I thought you might like to go for a swim and then we can get some lunch.'

'You should have seen what we found, Uncle Digby,' Clementine burst out.

Freddy nudged her and frowned.

'What was it?' the old man asked.

'I can't tell you because it's a secret,' she said.

'Oh, I see,' Uncle Digby said seriously as he tried not to smile.

FISH AND CHIPS

'I can't remember the last time I had fish and chips on the beach,' Aunt Violet said as she waved a plump chip in the air.

Uncle Digby had taken Clementine and Freddy to Mr Alessi's to buy fish and chips for their lunch. In the meantime, Lady Clarissa had returned to the beach. She had left Della at home with her grandmother, whining about her sore leg and sunburn.

Clementine watched a seagull that had landed close by. It was stalking around their camp.

Her great-aunt popped her chip into her mouth and reached for another. This time she wasn't quick enough. The cheeky grey-and-white gull raced in and plucked the tasty morsel from her fingertips.

'Good heavens!' Aunt Violet turned to face the feathered thief. 'Get away from me, you horrid beast.'

Everyone laughed. Lavender ran towards the bird, grunting and squealing.

Uncle Digby grinned. 'Perhaps you shouldn't wave your chips around like a conductor's baton, Miss Appleby.'

Aunt Violet leaned forward to protect her food. 'Thank you, Lavender – at least you're looking after me.' She offered the little pig a chip.

Fortunately, one of the Alessi Brothers' fishing boats puttered into the harbour a minute later. Every seagull on the beach flew over to see if any undersized treats would be thrown to them.

Just as the group finished their lunch, dark clouds rolled across the sky and thunder

rumbled out at sea. Lady Clarissa gathered up the towels. Even Aunt Violet pitched in by folding the chairs. Uncle Digby just managed to grab hold of the beach umbrella as the wind whipped it out of the sand.

'We'd best make a run for it,' Lady Clarissa called.

The group scrambled along the beach, up the steps and across the road. Lavender squealed and wriggled in Clementine's arms. Freddy ran down the garden path and pushed open the front door just as the rain began to belt down.

'Well, that was good timing,' Lady Clarissa puffed. She directed the children to rub the sand off their feet and legs before they entered the hall.

'Oh, there you are!' Mrs Dent rushed towards them. 'I was beginning to worry. Come and I'll get you some tea.'

'Is there somewhere I can put all this?' Uncle Digby was balancing the umbrella, the beach chairs and a pile of towels.

'There's a utility room at the end of the hall.'

Mrs Dent had the kettle on in no time and poured two glasses of orange juice for Clementine and Freddy.

'How's Della?' Lady Clarissa asked.

'The child has managed to get herself burnt to a crisp. Clearly she did not have sunscreen on this morning when I asked her. Now she's going to pay for it. In fact, I think she might have a touch of sunstroke,' Mrs Dent tutted.

'What about her leg?' Lady Clarissa asked.

Mrs Dent frowned. 'I think that was just some completely harmless seaweed. It might be a bit scratchy, but that's all. Anyway, how was the rest of your day?'

'It was great!' Clementine exclaimed. 'We made some new friends and we went exploring and we found –'

'Crabs!' Freddy said, giving Clementine a secret look.

'Well, it sounds like you've had a very adventurous day, my dears,' Mrs Dent said as she hopped up to refill the teapot.

'And another five to go,' Clementine said.

Freddy's face fell. 'Only five?'

'We have to go home on Sunday,' said Clementine.

Freddy didn't ever want Clementine to go home. He wondered if Lady Clarissa would consider taking Della instead.

ESCAPE

The rain lashed the coast for hours. Freddy and Clementine played Old Maid in the kitchen. Mrs Dent cooked dinner while she and Uncle Digby chatted about their childhoods. Aunt Violet and Lady Clarissa read in the sitting room. Della stayed in her room. She didn't come down for dinner either. Mrs Dent took her a tray. She returned saying that the child was utterly miserable with her sunburn.

'Will the storm be gone by tomorrow?' Clementine asked Mrs Dent.

'It should be. Storms like this usually come in a fury and leave just as quickly.'

But Mrs Dent was wrong. The next morning, Clementine looked out her bedroom window and discovered a grey, dreary day.

'No beach today,' she sighed and turned to her mother, who was lying in bed.

'No, darling. But there are plenty of things you can do inside.'

Freddy and Clementine spent the morning playing board games in the sitting room with Uncle Digby and Lady Clarissa. Even Aunt Violet joined in for a round of Snakes and Ladders. Della stayed upstairs, ringing a bell constantly for her grandmother, until Mrs Dent stumped upstairs for the fifth time and brought the bell back down with her.

After lunch, Freddy and Clementine decided to do some drawing at the kitchen table. Clementine started drawing a picture of a seal, with great big brown eyes and little flippers.

'I think the ears are cute,' she said to Freddy. He was drawing an octopus strangling a crab.

'What do you think, Lavender?' Clementine held up her picture. The little pig looked up and grunted.

The kitchen door flew open and Della stalked into the room. 'Where's Granny?'

'I don't know,' Freddy said with a shrug.

'I want something to eat.' Della yanked open the refrigerator door and peered inside.

A huge fish stared up at her from a platter. 'Pooh! I hate fish.'

She slammed the door and went to the biscuit tin, where she found two chocolate brownies.

'Are you feeling better?' Clementine asked. The girl's face was bright red.

'Sort of,' Della said. She walked back to the table and stood beside Clementine, looking at the child's drawing.

'It's a seal,' Clementine said.

'I know that,' Della replied. She wasn't about to say so, but she thought it was a good picture for a five-year-old.

'I saw a seal at the beach,' Della bragged, before taking a big bite of brownie.

'When?' asked Freddy.

'You weren't there,' Della said.

'I don't believe you,' Freddy retorted. 'You've never seen a seal. But we have.' He clamped his hands over his mouth but it was too late. The words had already escaped.

Clementine looked at Freddy.

'When?' Della asked, narrowing her eyes.

Freddy ignored her and kept drawing.

'Now who's telling lies?' Della said smartly.

Clementine couldn't stay quiet any longer. 'He's not lying. We saw a seal in a cave yesterday, after you went home.'

'Really? Show me,' Della demanded.

'It probably won't be there any more,' Clementine said. 'But it was so sweet.'

'I want to see the seal,' Della said, stamping her foot.

Clementine looked out the kitchen window at the steely sky. 'It's raining.'

Della rolled her eyes. 'We've got raincoats. Come on.'

'I don't think Mummy will let me go out,' said Clementine. 'She's upstairs having a rest.'

'You're such a baby,' Della scoffed.

'She is not,' Freddy said, his eyebrows knitting together fiercely.

'You're both babies,' Della spat. 'I'm going to see this seal whether you come or not.'

'You won't even find it,' Freddy said, as his sister stormed out of the kitchen.

Clementine stared at Freddy. 'Are you going to tell your granny?'

Freddy shook his head. 'I don't care if she goes. She won't see anything. She didn't even take a torch.'

Both children went back to drawing. A few minutes later, Clementine glanced around the room. 'Where's Lavender?'

Freddy peered around the room too. 'I don't know. She was here before.'

Clementine slipped down from her chair and walked around the kitchen, searching beside the stove and under the table.

'She's not here,' Clementine said, frowning. She went into the hallway and glanced towards the front door. 'Freddy! Come quick!'

Freddy flew out of his seat and into the hall. The front door was wide open.

'Della!' he called and raced onto the porch.

The front gate was open too.

Clementine stared at the boy, her blue eyes wide. 'Come on. We've got to find Lavender.'

'Wait a minute.' Freddy ran back to the kitchen and grabbed his torch off the bench.

STUCK

The sky was still dark but it had stopped raining. Clementine and Freddy ran out the front gate and across the road to the beach. Clementine's voice rang out. 'Lavender? Lavender!'

Freddy echoed the call.

'She probably followed Della,' he said eventually. 'Don't worry. She can't have gone too far yet.'

Clementine nodded. She hoped he was right.

Freddy looked down to the little beach but it was bare. He and Clementine ran along the wet sand towards the rocks.

'Be careful, Clementine, it's slippery,' the boy warned as they scrambled over the platform.

'Della, where are you?' Freddy called.

'Lavender!' Clementine shouted. She turned around and was relieved to see a little grey figure dashing towards them. Clementine scooped the pig into her arms and kissed the top of her head.

'Thank goodness,' Freddy sighed.

'What about Della?' Clementine asked. 'Do you think she's in the cave?'

'I don't know, but we could have a look.'

The two children picked their way around the headland, then leapt down across the little channel of water onto the tiny beach. Clementine gasped as she almost slipped in. She clutched Lavender tightly and looked back at the rising water. Freddy pulled the creeper back and shone the torchlight inside.

'Della!' he called. His voice echoed. *Della-ella-ella.*

The empty soft-drink bottles were still there but there was no sign of Della or the seal.

'She's not here,' Freddy said. 'We should go back before Granny gets worried.'

Clementine turned around. The sun was peeking through the clouds. The rocks looked shiny and clean and the grass that grew along the edge of the cliff was bright green.

'Freddy, look at the water. It's too high,' Clementine gulped. 'How can we get back?'

Freddy spun around. The little channel separating the curve of beach and the rock platform was filling fast. Water was starting to force its way into the cave as well.

'The tide's coming in,' he said.

'What does that mean?' asked Clementine. She was holding Lavender tight.

'The tide is the sea coming in and going out. The water gets deeper and shallower. But I think we can still get across now.'

Clementine shook her head. 'I'm scared. It's too deep. Is there another way?'

'No, that cliff's too steep. We can't get up there. But it's okay. The water never covers the whole beach. We can wait over there.' Freddy pointed to a grassy spot that met the sand at the end of the tiny beach. 'We're safe. I promise. But we won't be able to get across until the water goes down again.'

Clementine's eyes filled with tears. 'How long does that take?'

Freddy bit his lip. 'I don't know exactly.'

'But Mummy will be worried.' Fat tears began to flow down Clementine's cheeks. Lavender turned and licked the salty drops away.

'Don't worry, Clementine. Someone will come,' the boy said. But Freddy had a terrible feeling that it would be night-time before the tide went out again.

RESCUE

Freddy and Clementine climbed up onto the grassy knoll. Lavender was snorting and looking at the sea. Clementine's stomach was churning.

'Look, there's Della!' Freddy said.

His sister appeared on the top of the rock platform.

Della had thought Freddy would follow her when she stormed out to look for the seal. She hadn't wanted to go to that stinky cave on her own. It was much too dark and scary. But when the boy hadn't appeared she went for a walk around the village. Mrs Lee had given her an ice-cream, which she'd eaten while sitting on the seawall. Then she came to the beach to look for crabs in the rock pools.

'Della!' Freddy called above the sound of the waves.

She looked up and was surprised to see her brother and Clementine on the other side of the channel. 'What are you doing over there?' she called back.

'We're stuck,' the boy shouted.

Della's stomach tightened. Freddy might be a pain sometimes but she didn't want him to be stuck at high tide.

'Don't worry. I'll get help!' the girl shouted. She scurried back across the rocks to the beach.

Lady Clarissa had searched high and low for the children. She was about to go down and check the kitchen once more, when she met Uncle Digby.

'Hello dear,' he greeted her.

'You haven't seen Clementine, have you?'

The old man shook his head. 'Afraid I've been in the land of nod for the past couple of hours.'

Aunt Violet's bedroom door opened and the woman marched outside.

'Is this a party?' she asked her niece and Uncle Digby.

'I'm trying to find the children,' said Lady Clarissa.

'Don't worry. They're probably playing hide-and-seek or some such nonsense.'

Lady Clarissa didn't look convinced. 'It's far too quiet for my liking.'

The three adults walked down to the kitchen.

'Did you find them, dear?' Mrs Dent asked. Lady Clarissa shook her head.

The front door banged.

Mrs Dent breathed a sigh of relief. 'There

you go. They must have been in the garden.'

'Granny, Granny!' Della's voice rang through the house. The child raced into the kitchen.

'What's the matter?' Mrs Dent asked.

'Freddy and Clementine went to find the seal and now they're stuck,' the child blurted.

Aunt Violet pursed her lips. 'What seal?'

'Della, what nonsense are you talking about this time? Have you done something to your brother again?' Mrs Dent frowned.

Della shook her head. 'I promise, Granny, it's true. I'm not making it up.'

Uncle Digby nodded. 'The children did tell me they'd found a cave yesterday.'

'And now the tide's coming in and they're stuck on the tiny beach,' insisted Della.

Lady Clarissa caught her breath. 'What do you mean they're stuck?'

'The water's coming into the channel and Clementine is too small to jump the rocks and she's got Lavender too,' Della blurted.

'Oh, goodness. Come on, Della. Show me,' said Lady Clarissa hurriedly.

'What about some rope?' Aunt Violet suggested. 'Just in case.'

Lady Clarissa stopped. 'That's a great idea, Aunt Violet.'

Mrs Dent rushed off down the hallway to the utility room, and returned with a tightly wound length of rope. She threw the bundle to Clarissa.

'Okay, let's go,' Lady Clarissa said.

Della took off, with Lady Clarissa, Aunt Violet, Uncle Digby and Mrs Dent in pursuit.

Lady Clarissa shouted over her shoulder, 'Uncle Digby, please don't rush.'

'Yes, don't overdo it, Pertwhistle,' said Aunt Violet. 'We don't need you having another trip to the hospital.'

A few minutes later, Lady Clarissa and Della reached the rock shelf. The surf was much bigger than the day before and every couple of minutes a shower sprayed over the ledge.

'Mummy!' Clementine shouted.

'Oh, darling, I'm here,' Lady Clarissa called back. She looked at the little channel, which was getting deeper by the second.

Uncle Digby and the others arrived just as Lady Clarissa was tying the rope securely around her middle.

'Take this.' She handed the end to Uncle Digby.

'Oh, do be careful, Clarissa,' said Aunt Violet, her voice fluttering.

'I think we should all hold on,' Uncle Digby said.

Mrs Dent wrapped her hands around Uncle Digby's waist and Aunt Violet did the same to Mrs Dent. The three of them formed an anchor.

Lady Clarissa stepped down onto the rocks. Water swirled around her feet and she waded into the rushing tide.

'Come as close as you can, sweetheart, and I'll take Lavender first,' Lady Clarissa directed.

Clementine did as she was told and within a minute Lavender was safely on the other side in Della's arms.

'Come on, darling, you're next,' Clarissa urged Clementine towards her. 'Stay there, Freddy. I'll be back for you in a minute.'

'I'm okay,' Freddy called.

Clementine turned and looked at her friend.

'Go on,' he said. 'You'll be all right.'

Clementine reached out towards her mother. Lady Clarissa grabbed Clementine's hand and hauled her across the swirling water. She hugged the child tight.

'I'm sorry, Mummy, I'm sorry,' Clementine sobbed.

Clarissa passed her to Uncle Digby before wading in for the third time. She reached out and grabbed Freddy's hands. Together they scrambled up the rocks to safety.

'Goodness me, whatever were you thinking coming out here on your own?' Aunt Violet admonished the pair.

'I'm just glad you're safe,' Mrs Dent said, giving Freddy a hug.

'We would have been okay,' said Freddy. 'It might have been a bit scary in the dark, that's all.'

'Well, you're lucky Della found you,' Mrs Dent said. 'If that's what really happened.'

Della looked sheepish.

'Della?' Mrs Dent's tone was not to be messed with.

'It's my fault,' Della said, a tear rolling down her cheek.

Freddy and Clementine looked at each other in surprise.

'I said that Freddy and Clementine were babies because they wouldn't take me to see the seal and so I went on my own. But I was too scared. I went to the village instead and then I came to look at the rock pools,' Della said, sniffling.

Lady Clarissa looked at Freddy and Clementine. 'But why did you come here, if you'd already told Della you wouldn't?'

'Because Lavender escaped and we thought she'd followed Della to the cave,' Clementine explained.

Mrs Dent looked at her granddaughter, a swell of disappointment rising in her chest. 'Did you let Lavender out on purpose?'

'No, Granny. I promise I didn't. I thought

I pulled the door shut. But I remember I left the gate open,' Della sniffed. 'I'm sorry. I really am. I love Freddy. He's my brother.'

Aunt Violet looked at Freddy and winked. 'Well, young man, I bet that's not something you hear every day.'

Freddy grinned.

'Did you really find a seal yesterday?' Uncle Digby asked, breaking the tension.

Clementine nodded. She brushed the tears from her eyes and glanced back towards the cave.

As the group had been talking, the tide had risen much higher. Water was now rushing in and out of the little cave.

'Look,' Clementine cried out. 'There it is!'

'You really *did* find a seal!' Della said, her face crumpling into a smile.

The group was amazed to see a little seal bobbing up and down right in front of them. He swam into the cave and shot back out again as fast as a bullet. Then he rolled over and raised his flipper in the air.

Clementine grinned. 'Did that seal just wave at us?'

'I think he did, Clemmie,' Uncle Digby nodded. 'I think he did.'

CAST OF CHARACTERS

The Appleby household

Clementine Rose Appleby	Five-year-old daughter of Lady Clarissa
Lavender	Clemmie's teacup pig
Lady Clarissa Appleby	Clementine's mother and the owner of Penberthy House
Digby Pertwhistle	Butler at Penberthy House
Aunt Violet Appleby	Clementine's grandfather's sister

Pharaoh	Aunt Violet's beloved sphynx cat

Others

Mrs Rosamund Dent	Owner of the Endersley-on-Sea guesthouse
Della Dent	Mrs Dent's granddaughter
Freddy Dent	Mrs Dent's grandson
Lenny Phipps	Tow-truck driver
Alice-Miranda Highton-Smith Kennington-Jones	A new friend
Millie	A new friend
Jacinta	A new friend

CLEMENTINE ROSE
and the Treasure Box

Jacqueline Harvey

RANDOM HOUSE AUSTRALIA

For Ian and Darcy, Flynn,
Eden and Baby Lawrence

NEW NEIGHBOURS

Clementine Rose chased the ball as it bumped and rolled across the front lawn. Lavender, her teacup pig, scurried along beside her, grunting and squealing. Clementine reached the ball first. She stopped it with her foot and then kicked it back towards Uncle Digby. Lavender spun around and ran after it.

'You two are going to be exhausted,' said Clementine's mother, Lady Clarissa Appleby. She was pulling weeds from the flowerbed beside the fence.

'I know,' Clementine puffed. 'Lavender will need a big rest this afternoon.'

Lady Clarissa grinned. 'I meant you and Uncle Digby, darling.'

'Oh,' said Clementine, giggling.

'I'm all right,' the old man protested with a flick of his hand.

'Well, I think I'm just about done here,' said Lady Clarissa. She dumped a giant clump of clover into the hessian sack beside her.

Digby rolled the ball gently towards Lavender, who pushed it along with her snout. 'You know, that pig's a natural with a soccer ball.'

'Maybe she can join our team,' said Clementine. 'You could too, Uncle Digby.'

Clementine couldn't wait to start soccer in a few weeks' time. She was going to be on a team with her friends Poppy and Sophie, and some boys too. Sophie's father, Pierre, had offered to be the coach and they would play in a local Saturday morning competition.

The old man shook his head. 'I don't think so, Clementine. I'm about sixty-five years too old to be playing in the Under 7s.' He walked over to Clarissa and reached for the sack. 'I'll take those weeds around to the bin.'

'Thank you,' said Clarissa. She removed her gloves and brushed some dirt from her skirt.

'Do you want to kick with me, Mummy?' Clementine asked.

'Maybe later, sweetheart. I think we should pop inside and have something to eat.'

The front door opened and Clementine's great-aunt walked out onto the steps. 'When's lunch, Clarissa? A person could starve to death in this house,' she harrumphed.

Lady Clarissa rolled her eyes at Clementine. 'We're coming now, Aunt Violet. I don't suppose you thought to make a start on some sandwiches?'

Aunt Violet winced. 'I wouldn't know where to begin.'

'It's not that hard,' Clementine chimed in. 'You just have to get the bread and butter and some things to put inside. I'll teach you.'

'Stop being so practical, Clementine. Some people were born to cook and others were born to eat. Clearly I fall into the latter category.'

Clementine wondered what that meant.

'Why don't you get your ball and bring Lavender inside, darling,' Lady Clarissa suggested.

Lavender had nudged the ball all the way across the lawn. Now it was stuck under some bushes by the low stone wall that separated Penberthy House from the road. Just as Clementine bent down to pick up the ball, a truck rumbled past. There were large letters written on the side and three men sitting in the front.

Lady Clarissa looked at the vehicle. A young fellow wearing a blue singlet grinned and waved at her. Clarissa raised her hand and waved back.

Clementine grabbed her soccer ball and raced over to her mother, who had joined Aunt Violet on the front porch.

'What did it say on the truck?' she asked.

'Griffin Brothers Removals,' Lady Clarissa informed her.

A silver station wagon turned into the road and followed the truck. A woman waved from the front passenger seat. Clarissa thought she saw some children in the back.

'They must be the new neighbours,' she said.

Clementine's eyes grew wide.

There was only one other dwelling past Penberthy House, a cottage at the very end of the lane.

'Godfathers, who'd want to live in that dump?' Aunt Violet said with a shudder.

Clementine shook her head. 'It's not a dump any more, Aunt Violet. It's lovely.'

'I can't imagine it. No one's lived there since I was a girl,' the old woman replied.

It was true that the place had been abandoned for years. Weeds and creepers had wrapped around the cottage's whitewashed walls, poking their way through cracks in the floorboards and into the house. The rafters were full of birds' nests and a family of rabbits had made itself at home in one of the kitchen cupboards. But that was before the builders had arrived.

Uncle Digby and Clementine had walked down to take a look at the progress the previous weekend. The house had been extended, re-roofed and repainted. Sitting in its pretty, tamed garden, it seemed as good as new.

Clementine looked up at her mother. 'Do you think there'll be any children?'

'I can't say for sure, but I thought I saw some in the back of the car,' Clarissa replied.

Clementine danced about on the spot. 'Can we go and visit them, Mummy? Please?'

'Not today, sweetheart,' said Clarissa. 'We need to give the family some time to get unpacked and settled. Maybe we can take them a cake tomorrow to welcome them to the village.'

Clementine felt as if she might burst. 'I'll help make it. It should be chocolate with sprinkles and chocolate icing.'

'Settle down, Clementine. They're only neighbours,' Aunt Violet said, rolling her eyes. 'The last family I remember living there had two of the most horrible brats I've ever known. They used to steal apples from the trees in our garden and their dog was always up here making a nuisance of itself. It would leave steaming messages all around the place.'

Clementine frowned. 'What do you mean, Aunt Violet?'

The old woman arched an eyebrow. 'Think about it, Clementine – have you ever seen a dog writing a note? What sort of messages do they leave?'

Clementine realised what her great-aunt was talking about and giggled. 'Oh. But we don't even know if this family has a dog.'

'Well, we can jolly well hope not,' Aunt Violet said with a grimace.

But Clementine would be very happy to have some children close by. Her two best friends from school lived in Highton Mill, and even then Poppy was on a farm a way out of the village. It would be lovely to have someone to play with after school.

'Come on, Clemmie, let's get those sandwiches,' called Lady Clarissa, as she walked through the front door.

Aunt Violet marched in behind her. 'A cup of tea would be nice too.'

Clementine lingered on the porch a little longer. She didn't care what Aunt Violet said. She couldn't wait to meet the neighbours.

CAKE MIX

Clementine licked the spatula, smearing cake batter around her mouth. She scraped the bowl one last time before Lady Clarissa scooped it up and popped it in the sink.

'But, Mummy, I wasn't finished,' Clementine protested.

'You were about to take the colour off that bowl, young lady,' her mother said with a grin. 'Besides, the cake will be ready soon and we still have to make the icing.'

'Can I help?' Clementine asked.

'Of course.'

The tantalising aroma of warm chocolate cake filled the kitchen.

Uncle Digby arrived back from Mrs Mogg's store. He placed a small pile of letters on the bench and then began to unpack the grocery bag.

'Hello Uncle Digby,' Clementine said.

'Hello. Something smells delicious,' said the old man. 'I think these are for you.' He handed Clementine a packet of chocolate sprinkles.

'Thank you. Do you want to come meet the neighbours this afternoon?' Clementine asked.

'I'm afraid I can't. I have quite a bit to do. We have lots of guests arriving this weekend.'

The timer on the bench dinged and Clementine leapt down from her chair. 'It's ready!'

'Hold on, Clemmie,' said Clarissa, as she reached for a pair of oven mitts and opened the oven door. She pulled the shelf towards her and plunged a skewer into the middle of the cake. It came out clean.

'All done,' Clementine sang.

Lady Clarissa placed the tin on the cooling rack on the bench. 'We can mix the icing now. Then when we're finished, the cake should be just about cool enough to decorate.'

A little while later, Clementine finished shaking sprinkles onto the chocolate icing while her mother searched the pantry for a cake box.

'Are you coming to meet the neighbours, Aunt Violet?' Clementine asked the old woman, who had wandered into the kitchen in search of a cup of tea and was now reading the newspaper.

She shook her head. 'You can meet them first. And don't go inviting them for dinner or any such nonsense, Clarissa. We don't know anything about them. Probably not our sort of people at all.'

Clementine wondered who their sort of people were but decided not to ask. Aunt Violet was in a bit of a scratchy mood already.

Lady Clarissa told Clementine to run along and fetch a cardigan and give her hair a quick brush. The child scampered up the back stairs and returned a couple of minutes later.

'Can we take Lavender?' she asked, as she walked over to give the little pig a rub. Lavender and Pharaoh, Aunt Violet's sphynx cat, were in their usual position: snuggled together in Lavender's basket in front of the cooker.

'No, darling. We should see if the new family has any pets first. We wouldn't want to take Lavender and have her upset anyone, would we?' her mother replied.

Clementine nodded. That was probably the best idea.

A few minutes later the pair set off. It was about half a mile to the cottage. The pretty lane was bounded by a low stone wall on one side and open fields on the other. A trio of black-and-white cows grazed in the field. One looked up and mooed at Clementine, who mooed back.

'What if they're not home?' Clementine asked.

'Well, we can just leave the cake on the doorstep. At least we've had a nice walk.'

'But what if a sheep eats the cake?'

'A sheep? Which sheep?' her mother asked.

'Any sheep.' Clementine said. 'Sheep eat cake, you know. Just look at Ramon, the ram at Poppy's farm. He loves chocolate brownies.'

Her mother laughed. 'Clementine, some-times you do say the strangest things.'

Clementine looked up at her mother and shrugged. 'It's true.'

They rounded the bend at the bottom of the road and, sure enough, the silver station wagon that had driven past the day before was parked in the driveway.

Clementine opened the front gate and ran down the path to the little porch. She looked at the door. There was no bell, only a brass lion's head knocker. She reached up and banged three times.

NEW FRIENDS

After a few moments, the door opened and a tall, thin man with a pointy brown beard and black-framed glasses looked at Clemmie. He had curly brown hair and wore checked pants and a dark-blue waistcoat over a white shirt with the sleeves rolled up.

'Hello,' he said, glancing from Clementine to her mother.

'Hello, I'm Clarissa Appleby and this is my daughter Clementine Rose. We live just up the road in –'

'Penberthy House,' the fellow finished. He had a huge grin on his face.

'Yes,' Clarissa said, smiling. 'Welcome to Penberthy Floss.'

'We're thrilled to be here,' the man said, nodding. 'And we're *thrilled* to meet you.'

Clementine pointed at the box in her mother's hands. 'We made a cake.'

'You must come in and have tea,' he said.

'We don't want to interrupt,' Lady Clarissa said. 'You must be terribly busy unpacking.'

Clementine frowned. 'But Mummy, you said that we couldn't come yesterday because they would be unpacking and that's why we had to wait until today.' She feared that her mother was going to turn around and head home. Clementine was dying to find out if there were any children in the house.

'No, we're glad to have a reason to stop.' He turned and called into the house, 'Ana, darling, put the kettle on. We have guests.'

Lady Clarissa and Clementine followed the man down the hallway. They skirted around packing boxes piled high, past a staircase, and through another door at the end of the passageway.

They stopped in a beautiful kitchen and family room. It was surrounded by windows with a view of the back garden.

'Ana,' the man said. A tall woman spun around from the sink with a kettle in her hand.

'Hello there,' she said, smiling.

Clementine thought she was one of the prettiest ladies she'd ever seen. Her blue eyes sparkled and her dark hair was pulled back into a sleek bun.

'Hello,' Lady Clarissa said.

'Oh my heavens, I haven't even told you my name.' The man hit the heel of his hand against his forehead. 'You must think me a real twit.'

'Of course not,' Lady Clarissa said. 'I can understand why you'd be distracted.'

'I'm Basil Hobbs and this is my wife Anastasia,' he said with an embarrassed grin.

'Please, everyone calls me Ana.' The woman switched on the kettle and lined up several mugs on the stone bench.

'It's lovely to meet you. I'm Clarissa Appleby and this is my daughter Clementine Rose,' Clarissa replied.

'We made you a cake,' Clementine said as her mother handed the box to Ana.

The woman lifted the lid. 'Oh, it looks delicious. The children are going to love this.'

Clementine's blue eyes widened. 'What children?'

'We have three, Clementine,' the woman replied.

An excited tingle ran down Clementine's spine.

'Our eldest, Araminta, is almost eleven, and the twins, Tilda and Teddy, are about to turn six.'

Clementine beamed. 'That's the same as me.'

'Actually, Basil, it's awfully quiet. Do you know where they are?' Ana asked.

'I think they've gone to see what Flash

thinks of the creek,' he replied. 'I'll give them a shout.'

'Who's Flash?' Clementine asked.

'He's the twins' tortoise,' Ana said. 'He's an adorable little creature. I must admit I never thought a tortoise would be affectionate or interesting but he's both.'

Basil opened a glass door that led out onto a deck. 'Mintie, Tilda, Teddy,' he called. 'Come out, come out, wherever you are. We have guests and they brought cake!'

'The house is beautiful,' said Clarissa as she looked around the room admiringly. 'And this kitchen is gorgeous. What a dream.'

'Thank you. We're very pleased with how it all came up, especially as we weren't here for the renovation.' Ana noticed the puzzled look on Clarissa's face. 'We've been away for months. Basil was making a documentary in France so we decided we'd take the chance to travel with the children. It won't be long until Araminta is off to boarding school.'

'How wonderful,' Clarissa said. 'The travel,

not that your daughter's going to boarding school.'

'Oh, she can't wait. We've got her a place at the new secondary school at Winchesterfield-Downsfordvale but she has another year in primary first. The children are all off to Ellery Prep this year.'

'The same as me,' Clementine said with a big smile.

Basil walked back across the deck. 'They're coming now.'

There was a flash of brunette hair and gangly limbs. Three children tumbled into the kitchen. They regained their composure and looked at the visitors.

'Hello,' the older girl said. 'I'm Mintie. It's short for Araminta.'

Clementine smiled at her. She had long chocolate-brown hair and blue eyes like her mother's. She was tall like her parents too.

'My friend Sophie has a cat called Mintie,' Clementine said.

'Good choice,' the girl said with a smile.

The twins were about the same height as Clemmie and had dark hair too. The girl's hair was tied up in two pigtails and the boy's was short and wavy but not curly like his father's. They both had brown eyes.

'I'm Tilda and he's Teddy,' the younger girl said, looking at her brother.

'But my real name's Edward,' the boy explained.

Clementine was wondering if the girl had a different name too. She must have read Clementine's mind.

'And my name really is Tilda and I don't like anything else.' She nodded decisively.

'You look the same,' Clementine said. 'Except for your hair.'

'I'm five minutes older,' Teddy said proudly. 'So she's the baby of the family.'

'Everyone knows the youngest is the cutest.' Tilda grinned.

Araminta wrinkled her nose. 'Says who?'

'Says your apparently very cute little sister,' Basil said, rolling his eyes playfully.

Clementine liked the family already. She looked at the patterned shell in Tilda's hands. It was about the size of a bread and butter plate.

'This is Flash. He's a bit shy sometimes,' said Tilda. Clementine could just see the curve of the tortoise's neck hidden inside his portable home. 'He's still getting used to things but he'll come out when he's ready.'

Tilda put Flash into a basket on the floor in the corner of the kitchen. 'That's not his real house. We've got to find it. We don't know where the men from the truck put it.'

'This is Clarissa Appleby and Clementine Rose,' Basil said. 'They're our neighbours.'

'Hello everyone,' Clarissa said. 'It's lovely to meet you all.'

'Do you live in that massive house near the corner?' Araminta asked.

Clementine nodded.

'Wow!' the twins said in unison. 'That's a mansion.'

'Are there ghosts?' Teddy asked.

'I don't think so,' Lady Clarissa replied.

Tilda's eyes widened. 'What about in the attic?'

Lady Clarissa shook her head. 'I'm afraid not.'

'Really?' The girl wrinkled her lip. 'I thought all old houses had ghosts.'

'Sorry to disappoint you,' Lady Clarissa said.

'I'm not disappointed.' Araminta shuddered. She wasn't keen on anything spooky. Tilda and Teddy knew it and loved trying to scare their big sister.

'Sometimes I think Granny and Grandpa are like ghosts,' Clementine said. 'I imagine that they fly down from their portraits and take tea in the sitting room. Grandpa loves poetry and Granny is always smiling.'

The twins looked at each other. 'Cool!' they said at the same time.

Araminta shook her head. 'Not cool.' But she couldn't help thinking that Clementine was just about the cutest girl she'd ever met.

Basil opened the cake box and lifted the chocolate confection onto a plate.

Tilda licked her lips when she saw it. 'Yum.'

The group settled around the table with cups of tea for the adults and lemonade for the children.

'How did you ever come to buy this place?' Lady Clarissa asked, before taking a sip of her tea.

'We've been looking for a home in the country for quite a while now. A friend told us he'd seen a little cottage for sale in Penberthy Floss,' said Basil. A sheepish look settled on the man's face. 'I have to admit I knew the village because of your house.'

'Our house?' Lady Clarissa asked in surprise.

'I make documentaries about grand homes, and Penberthy House has been on my list for ages, along with Highton Hall and Lord Tavistock's pile.'

Lady Clarissa laughed. 'I'm afraid our place is nothing like either of those mansions.'

'Perhaps not, but I'm sure that it has just as fascinating a history.'

'You're probably right about that,' said Lady Clarissa, nodding.

The adults continued chatting about the house while the children drank their lemonade and tucked into their cake.

'This is good!' Teddy said as crumbs sputtered from his mouth.

Clementine smiled.

'Do you have any pets?' Araminta asked. 'Daddy said that we're going to get a dog now that we live in the country.'

Clementine stiffened. She hoped it wasn't a dog that liked to leave messages. Aunt Violet would definitely have something to say about that.

'I have a teacup pig,' said Clementine. 'Her name is Lavender and she's at home with Pharaoh. He's Aunt Violet's cat.'

'A teacup pig!' Tilda and Teddy said at exactly the same time.

Araminta looked at the twins and shook her head. 'They always do that,' she explained to Clementine. 'You'll get used to it even though it can be a bit weird.'

The children fired a volley of questions at Clementine about where she went to school and what sort of things there were to do in the village and if she had a pony. They'd soon finished their afternoon tea and asked if they could take her on a tour of the house and garden.

'Yes, of course,' said Lady Clarissa. 'But we can't stay too long.'

'Aunt Violet will grumble if dinner is late,' Clementine said.

'Who's Aunt Violet?' Araminta asked.

'She's Grandpa's sister and she complains a *lot*,' Clementine explained.

'Clemmie, she's not that bad,' her mother said.

'Well, she was when she first came to stay and now she's never going to leave,' Clementine said. 'But I suppose we're used to her.'

The children scooted into the hallway and up the stairs, leaving Basil and Ana frowning and Lady Clarissa with a rueful smile on her face.

The children delighted in showing off every nook and cranny of the house, including a wonderful space in the attic with a whole lot of mirrors.

Clementine pointed to a long barre running along the mirrored wall. 'What's that for?'

'That's Mummy's, so she can practise,' Tilda said.

'Practise what?' Clementine asked.

'Ballet. She's going to start a ballet school in the village hall,' Araminta explained.

Clementine's eyes widened. 'I love ballet.'

'Maybe you can join Mummy's school. She's very good at it. I helped her choose the tutus that the girls will have to wear. They're red,' said Tilda.

'Do you learn?' she asked the children.

Araminta shook her head. 'I used to but I didn't really like it.'

'We do,' the twins said together.

Clementine's tummy fluttered. The twins shared a room and Araminta had her own with a bathroom between them. There was another room, which their father was planning to use as a study, and their parents' bedroom, which had a smart white ensuite with a beautiful big bath. Clementine thought Aunt Violet would have liked that a lot.

The foursome darted back downstairs and took Clementine into the garden. A lush lawn rolled down to a little creek. The children passed the raised garden beds, which were for a new vegetable patch.

'Uncle Felix said that he's going to build us a tree house up there.' Tilda pointed into the fork of an ancient oak. 'Daddy can't build anything but Uncle Felix can build everything. He fixed the house.'

'That would be amazing,' Clementine said. She loved the idea of having a tree house to play in.

A little while later, Basil called out that it was time for Clementine to go. The children were inspecting the newly constructed chicken coop, which was waiting for some residents. They raced back to the house.

'Mummy, there's a chicken house and their uncle is going to build a tree house and there's a play room in the attic, with a barre and mirrors for ballet,' Clementine said excitedly. 'Can they come and play tomorrow?' She looked at her mother, her blue eyes pleading.

'Of course, darling, if it's all right with Basil and Ana,' Clarissa replied.

'How about I walk them up after lunch?' Basil suggested.

'I can give you a tour of the house if you like?' Clarissa said.

Basil rubbed his pointy little beard and grinned. 'Oh, that would be splendid.'

'Why don't you all come for afternoon tea?' Clarissa said. 'Say, two o'clock.'

'You can meet Aunt Violet,' said Clementine, wrinkling her nose. 'And Uncle Digby. He's lovely.'

'Is he married to Aunt Violet?' Ana asked.

Clementine began to giggle. 'No way. Uncle Digby's much too smart for that.'

Lady Clarissa quickly explained who Uncle Digby was.

'Well, see you tomorrow,' Clarissa said as she and Clementine set off.

'See you tomorrow,' the children and their parents called back.

EMERGENCY!

That evening, Clementine talked non-stop about her new friends. Aunt Violet was out for the evening with Mrs Bottomley. It had come as a surprise to everyone that the two ladies had become friends after Clementine's class excursion to the farm. The pair had got lost after Mrs Bottomley was chased by a crazy goose called Eloise, and Aunt Violet had gone after them. Ever since, Aunt Violet and Mrs Bottomley had bonded each week over a game of bridge and a glass of brandy. It helped that they had a mutual dislike of children too.

Uncle Digby said it was just as well Aunt Violet was out, as she hadn't been very enthusiastic about the neighbours. She would probably be rather miffed about Clemmie's eagerness and her niece inviting them for afternoon tea.

'Mummy, my tummy feels fluttery,' said Clementine as Lady Clarissa tucked her into bed.

'Why do you think that is?'

'Maybe because . . . it's excited. The children are so lovely and Ana is beautiful, isn't she?' Clementine said as her mother stroked her hair. 'Can I have ballet lessons, Mummy? Please.'

'We'll see about that. And, yes, Ana is beautiful and the children are fun, and Basil's a bit of a character. I think we're very lucky to have the Hobbses as neighbours.' She leaned down and kissed Clemmie's cheek.

'I'm going to tidy up my room in the morning,' Clementine said.

Lady Clarissa looked around. Clementine's room was never particularly messy at all. 'Why do you need to do that?'

'So I can show the kids,' Clementine said. 'Then I can help you.'

'Ah,' said Lady Clarissa. Clementine clearly wanted ballet lessons a lot. 'You're very sweet. Love you.' Lady Clarissa stood up and walked over to the door and flicked off the light.

'Love you too, Mummy.' Clementine closed her eyes and within a few minutes she was fast asleep.

Hours later, just after the grandfather clock downstairs chimed three, Clementine woke up and realised she needed the toilet. The house was quiet except for the usual creaks and groans. Lady Clarissa said that the new roof would probably make all sorts of noises for a while. Clementine slipped out of bed and plodded across the hall to the bathroom, still half-asleep. As she washed her hands, she glanced through the sheer curtains and wondered about the red glow across the field. Clementine rubbed her eyes and pulled the curtain back.

'Mummy!' she yelled. 'Mummy! Come quickly.'

Lady Clarissa had been sound asleep. So had Uncle Digby and Aunt Violet. But within a minute the three of them bumped into each other on the landing.

'Goodness, Clementine, you'll wake the dead with that bellowing,' Aunt Violet grumbled.

Lady Clarissa pushed open the bathroom door. 'What's the matter, Clemmie?'

'Look!' She pointed out the window.

Lady Clarissa focused. Uncle Digby pulled his glasses out of his dressing-gown pocket.

'Good heavens,' he said. 'I'll call the brigade.' He raced out to the telephone on the small table near the top of the stairs.

Aunt Violet peered through the window, her eyes adjusting to the light. 'Oh, oh dear. I wonder what it is. Don't just stand there, Clarissa. We should see if there's anything we can do.'

'Aunt Violet, I don't think we'll be much help,' said Lady Clarissa.

'Godfathers, Clarissa, don't be so dull. It's the most exciting thing to happen around here for a jolly long time and I'm not about to miss it,' the old woman sniffed.

Clementine was dancing about. She wanted to see what was happening too.

'Well don't just stand there, Clementine. Get your dressing-gown,' Aunt Violet insisted.

The child rushed back across the hall to her bedroom. She pulled her dressing-gown from the end of her bed and dragged it over her arms, then stuffed her feet into her slippers.

Clementine hurried downstairs with her mother close behind her. Uncle Digby was in the entrance hall but Aunt Violet had disappeared.

'Has she gone to get a bucket?' Digby asked. 'I'll get the car keys.'

The wailing of sirens in the distance signalled that the fire truck was on its way from Highton Mill.

Aunt Violet thumped downstairs and elbowed Digby out of the way. 'I'll drive! We're not taking that clapped-out bomb of yours.'

Aunt Violet's shiny red car was parked out the front of the house. A minute later, everyone was strapped into their seats. The back wheels spun as Aunt Violet planted her foot on the accelerator. The car hurtled down the driveway, out onto the street and around the corner to the village.

'Look out!' Clementine called as the fire truck raced past. Aunt Violet swerved out of the way.

'Maniacs! We could have been killed,' Aunt Violet huffed.

'Aunt Violet. That's the fire brigade.' Clementine shook her head. 'You have to get out of their way.'

Aunt Violet followed the truck past Mrs Mogg's store and the church.

'What's on fire?' she asked, squinting to see.

'Oh no!' Lady Clarissa gasped.

'Well, what is it?' Aunt Violet demanded.

'It's the village hall,' Clarissa replied.

Aunt Violet pulled a face. 'Is that all?'

'Don't sound so disappointed, Miss Appleby,'

Digby said from the back seat. He'd just managed to right himself and remove the seatbelt from around his neck. 'What were you hoping for? Mrs Mogg's shop? The village inn, or some poor soul's home?'

'Don't be ridiculous, Pertwhistle!' Aunt Violet retorted. 'I just meant that I'm glad it's nothing important.'

'The village hall *is* important, Aunt Violet,' Clementine said from the back seat. 'That's where we have the flower show and the village concert and where Ana was going to start her ballet school.'

'Who's Ana?' Aunt Violet asked.

Clementine began to explain but was interrupted.

'Does the woman have any experience?' Aunt Violet asked. 'Ballet is an art form. If you're not trained properly you can do all sorts of damage.'

'Did you do ballet, Aunt Violet?'

'Yes, of course. I took lessons when I was at boarding school. You don't get to have my posture without years of training. We have to see whether this Ana woman knows what she's talking about. I'll insist on seeing her references.'

Clementine was no longer listening. They'd stopped behind the fire truck, and she was watching as the firemen rolled out their hoses and began pumping water onto the flames. Clarissa opened the passenger door. The sirens had woken the whole village and a small crowd was gathering on the footpath across the street.

Clementine hopped out too. She'd never seen so many people in pyjamas before. It was a bit like a sleepover, except everyone was awake. She was surprised to see Mrs Mogg's hair in rollers and Father Bob in his dressing-gown, which had trains on it.

'Please stand back, everyone,' the fire captain called. As he spoke the roof collapsed, sending a shower of sparks into the air.

'Oh!' the crowd gasped.

The villagers watched on, murmuring to one another, mesmerised by the inferno. After a

while the flames began to die down. The smoke was starting to clear and it was obvious there was not a lot left of the hall.

Another siren wailed and a few minutes later a police car pulled up in the middle of the road. Two men got out and talked to the fire captain, and then one of them turned around to address the crowd.

He consulted his notepad. 'Is Digby Pertwhistle here?'

The old man raised his hand and stepped forward. 'Yes, that's me.'

'You reported the fire, is that correct?' the policeman asked.

'Yes, that's right. But it was Clementine who spotted it first,' Digby said.

Clementine stepped forward next to Uncle Digby. 'I saw the flames when I went to the toilet. Mummy said that I shouldn't have such a big glass of milk before bedtime but I was thirsty.'

'Well, it's just as well you did, young lady,' the policeman said, 'or else this fire might have been much worse. It looks like they've saved the old stables and the shed at the back.'

'Clementine, thank goodness you saw it.' Mrs Mogg rushed forward and enveloped the child. 'I was sleeping like a brick. I didn't hear a thing until the siren was right outside the front door.'

'Yes, well spotted, Clemmie,' Father Bob said.

Clementine shrugged. 'I just went to the toilet.'

The flames were almost out, with some smouldering embers keeping the firemen busy. The other policeman was attaching blue-and-white tape to the fence to indicate that the grounds were off limits.

'Did anyone see anything?' the first policeman asked the group.

There was a collective shaking of heads.

'No, but come to think of it, after our quilting club meeting last night, the light switch sparked on me as I turned it off to leave,' Mrs Mogg said with a frown. 'Goodness, I hope I wasn't the cause.'

The policeman nodded. 'Mmm, sounds like it could have been an electrical fault.'

'You couldn't have known there was a problem, Margaret,' Lady Clarissa said to the woman. She turned to Clementine. 'I think we should be getting home.'

Clarissa and Clemmie bade goodnight to Mrs Mogg and Father Bob and the other residents. Aunt Violet had run back to the car as soon as she had seen how many people were about. She didn't know what she'd been thinking arriving in her dressing-gown.

'Where's Pertwhistle?' Aunt Violet demanded as Clemmie and Clarissa climbed into the car.

'Uncle Digby said that it would be safer to walk home,' Clementine said.

'Did he now? Well, he can remember that the next time he wants a lift anywhere,' Aunt Violet said through pursed lips.

'But he never goes anywhere in the car with you,' Clementine said. 'Except for tonight.'

'If he doesn't like my driving, then too bad.' Aunt Violet pulled away from the kerb and did a U-turn, narrowly missing the police car.

'Godfathers! Why on earth is that parked there?' she grumbled and sped off into the night.

AFTER THE FIRE

Clementine rolled over and yawned. She wondered if the fire last night had been a dream. Then she remembered Aunt Violet's driving. That had been more like a nightmare.

There was a knock at her door and Lady Clarissa entered. 'Hello sleepyhead. You must have been tired.'

'I couldn't remember for a minute if the fire was real, but it was, wasn't it?' Clementine asked.

'Yes, darling. It was real. And so was that terrifying ride in Aunt Violet's car.'

Clementine sat up. 'Can we go to the village and have a look at the hall?'

Her mother nodded. 'I've got to get the mail and a few bits and pieces from Mrs Mogg. Hop up and get dressed. We'll go once you've had breakfast.'

'Tilda and Teddy and Mintie are coming for afternoon tea today, aren't they?' Clementine said suddenly. With everything else that had happened she'd almost forgotten about her new friends. 'Oh no! If there's no village hall, where will Ana have her ballet lessons?' Clementine's face fell. She'd been hoping that Mrs Mogg would be able to make her a tutu.

'I don't know, sweetheart, but I'm sure she will work something out. The Hobbses are a bit protected down in that hollow at the end of the road so they might not know about the fire yet. I'll break the news gently to Ana this afternoon.'

Lavender waddled into the room, snuffling along the floorboards. She'd already been downstairs and back again, having hopped out of her basket at the end of Clemmie's bed earlier when the girl was still sound asleep.

'Good morning, Lavender.' Clementine slipped down from her bed and cuddled the little pig.

Lady Clarissa opened the wardrobe door. 'What would you like to wear today?'

Clementine thought for a moment. 'May I please have the yellow dress with the blue flowers?'

'Lovely.' Her mother pulled the dress from the hanger. 'And Mrs Mogg will be so pleased to see you wearing it.'

Clementine's love of fashion was well known in the village. It was something she shared with her great-aunt. But while Aunt Violet spent hours poring over fashion magazines, it was Mrs Mogg who created all manner of outfits for the child. She enjoyed nothing more than spoiling Clementine with new clothes.

Clementine dressed and went downstairs to the kitchen. Aunt Violet was at the table, nibbling on some toast and flicking through a magazine.

'Good morning, Aunt Violet,' Clementine said.

The woman glanced up. 'Morning. That's a pretty dress.'

Clementine smiled. 'Mrs Mogg made it.'

'I wish she'd think about making some clothes in my size,' the old woman said with a frown. 'I'd love something new. But I suppose I'll just have to make do for now.'

Lady Clarissa came down the back stairs just in time to hear her aunt's gripe.

'Aunt Violet, you must have the largest collection of clothes on the planet. I'm almost certain you could wear something different every day for the next ten years,' Clarissa tutted.

'That's quite beside the point, Clarissa. I'd like something *new*.'

'Well, unless you win the lottery, you're just going to have to put up with what you've got.'

Clarissa pulled a box of cereal from the shelves and shook some flakes into a bowl.

Aunt Violet pointed a manicured finger towards her magazine. 'Look. There's a competition here to win an entire new wardrobe.'

'Well then, you should enter it,' Clarissa said.

'No, Mummy, *you* should enter it,' said Clementine. 'You're much luckier than Aunt Violet. She lost all her money and her house. And didn't you lose some of your husbands, too?' Clementine asked, glancing up at the woman.

'Clementine Rose Appleby, the cheek of you!' Aunt Violet jerked her chair back and stood up. 'It's all yours, Clarissa.' She pushed the magazine to the end of the table. 'And you'd better win. That might go some way towards making up for that insolent daughter of yours.' Aunt Violet stalked out of the room.

Clementine looked at her mother. 'Did I say something wrong? It was the truth, wasn't it?'

'Yes, darling. But sometimes grown-ups don't like to be reminded of their mistakes, that's all.' Clarissa poured some milk into the bowl and set it down on the table.

Clementine dug her spoon into the crispy flakes and took a mouthful.

GUESTS

s the grandfather clock struck two, the doorbell rang. Clementine and Lavender skittered out of the kitchen to the front hall.

Clementine wrenched open the door and saw Basil, Ana and their three children standing on the porch.

'Hello, please come in,' Clementine said. She made a slight bow. Lavender gave a small grunt.

'Thank you, Clementine.' Basil doffed his stylish trilby hat.

Ana smiled but the children only had eyes for Lavender. They were just about bursting with excitement.

'Oh my goodness, she's adorable!' Araminta exclaimed. 'Can I hold her?'

Clementine nodded and bent down to pick up the little pig.

She passed Lavender to Araminta, and the pig immediately snuggled against the girl's chest. Tilda scratched the creature under the chin and Lavender repaid her with a nibble.

Teddy jigged about excitedly. 'She's so cute. Mummy, can we have one?'

Ana shook her head. 'I thought we'd settled on a dog and some chooks, and we've already got Flash.'

Lady Clarissa came through the hall and joined them. 'Hello everyone. Welcome to Penberthy House.'

Basil was busily gazing about the foyer. His eyes came to rest on the Appleby family portraits lining the stairs.

'That's Granny and Grandpa,' said Clementine. She pointed at a regal-looking couple halfway up the wall. 'And that's Aunt Violet when she was young and beautiful. She's not like that any more.'

'I heard that, Clementine,' a sharp voice echoed from the upstairs landing.

'Oops!' Clementine covered her mouth and everyone exchanged grins.

'And what is going on down there?' Aunt Violet's head appeared over the banister rail.

'Aunt Violet, I'd like you to meet our new neighbours,' Lady Clarissa said.

'You didn't tell me you'd invited anyone over, Clarissa.' The old woman walked downstairs. 'Especially since I told you not to,' she muttered to herself.

'Aunt Violet.' Lady Clarissa's voice was stern. 'This is Basil and Ana Hobbs and their children Araminta, Teddy and Tilda.'

'Yes, yes, lovely to meet you all,' Aunt Violet said wanly. The old woman reluctantly shook hands with Basil, then looked at Ana. She studied the woman's face and it was as if a light came on. 'Oh my heavens. You're Anastasia Barkov.'

Ana nodded. 'That's what I was called professionally.'

'Good heavens, Clarissa, why didn't you tell me that our new neighbour is the recently retired prima ballerina of the Royal Ballet?' Aunt Violet demanded.

'I'm afraid I didn't know,' Lady Clarissa apologised.

'Please, I wouldn't have expected you to,' said Ana. Her ears and cheeks turned a matching shade of pink.

'The woman's a national icon, Clarissa. I suppose that's the trouble when you spend your life out here in the country, devoid of all culture,' Aunt Violet said. 'I myself love the ballet. If only I were able to get up to the city more often. I have a subscription, you know.'

Clarissa eyeballed her aunt. That subscription had been cancelled along with various other luxuries her aunt could no longer afford.

'No wonder you were planning on starting a ballet school,' Clementine said. 'But now the hall's burnt down.'

'The hall?' Basil queried, clearly unaware of the drama. 'When did that happen?'

'Last night,' Clementine said. 'There were huge flames and lots of smoke and a fire truck and everyone in their pyjamas. Mummy and I went for a walk this morning, and there's a big pile of burnt wood where the hall was.' She nodded emphatically.

'Oh dear,' said Ana. 'That's terrible.'

'Clementine, I thought we'd planned to break the news gently,' her mother said.

Clementine's face fell.

Ana noticed at once. 'It doesn't matter, Clementine. It might just delay my plans a little. I'm sure they'll rebuild the hall.'

'The rate anything happens around here, my dear, I wouldn't count on starting that school any time soon,' Aunt Violet said. 'Perhaps you'd be better off to find another venue.'

'I've already investigated lots of other

places and the Penberthy Floss Village Hall seemed to be the only space available. We'll just have to postpone, I suppose.'

Clementine didn't like that idea at all. She was keen to start ballet lessons as soon as possible.

'Please, why don't you all come and have something to eat,' Lady Clarissa suggested.

Digby Pertwhistle had just popped the kettle onto the stove when Clarissa appeared in the kitchen with the guests.

She quickly introduced him and asked that everyone take a seat. Clementine had to show the children Pharaoh first, of course.

'He looks weird,' Teddy whispered.

Clementine nodded. 'I know. He's a sphynx. They've got no hair. But he's lovable and he's Lavender's best friend apart from me.'

'What are you whispering about, Clementine?' Aunt Violet demanded.

'Nothing.' Clementine shook her head. She knew from experience that it was better not to comment aloud on Pharaoh's appearance.

'Why don't you show the children where to wash their hands, and then come and sit down,' Lady Clarissa suggested.

She placed a large strawberry sponge cake in the middle of the table. There was another platter of brownies to follow and some home-made honey jumbles too.

'Goodness me, Clarissa, you must be the world's best baker,' Ana commented.

'I can't take credit for all this. Pierre Rousseau owns the patisserie in Highton Mill. He delivers cakes and bread for Mrs Mogg to sell in the shop so I snapped up the sponge this morning. The brownies and honey jumbles are mine but they're a cinch.'

Clementine and the children returned and quickly sat down, eyeing off the tasty treats.

'That's still impressive,' said Ana. 'I don't cook.'

'Not at all?' Clarissa said.

'No. Basil is in charge of the food at our place. With all my touring and strict diets and the like, I'm sad to say it's not something

I've ever mastered. Maybe you could give me some lessons?'

'Of course not,' Aunt Violet said briskly. 'A performer such as yourself, dear, has no mind slaving over a hot stove. I don't believe in it either.'

'But you're not a ballerina, Aunt Violet,' Clementine said. 'You just don't like cooking.'

Aunt Violet wrinkled her lip and looked away. 'And what about you, Basil? What's your line of work?'

'I'm a filmmaker,' the man replied.

'Oh, fascinating.' Aunt Violet was paying the new neighbours far more attention than anyone might have imagined. 'Feature films?'

'Documentaries,' Basil said.

'Oh. How . . . educational.' Aunt Violet barely disguised her disappointment.

'Actually, I was thinking I'd like to make a film about Penberthy House,' Basil said.

'A film about our house?' Clementine asked, her eyes widening.

Aunt Violet's did too. 'Really?' A smug smile began to form.

'Well, I'm sure it has a wonderful history and from the little I've seen so far, the house seems mostly original.'

'That's just a polite way of saying "tatty", Basil,' Lady Clarissa said, smiling.

'No, not at all. This place is a gem and I'd love to uncover everything about it. Of course, I need your permission, Clarissa. I'd want to feature the family too,' Basil explained.

Uncle Digby looked at Lady Clarissa, who in turn looked towards Aunt Violet, who was preening her hair and looking very satisfied with herself.

'I don't know, Basil. We've always been quite a private family,' Lady Clarissa said.

'How can you say that, Clarissa?' Aunt Violet snapped. 'You've opened our beautiful home so that all the riffraff under the sun can stay here.'

'It could be very good for business, Clarissa,' said Uncle Digby.

'Yes, Mummy, imagine if we were on the

television. Lots of people would want to come and see Lavender and Pharaoh,' Clementine enthused.

'Can I have some time to think about it, Basil?' Lady Clarissa asked.

'Yes, of course. I'm busy for the next couple of months anyway. We couldn't start shooting for a while yet.'

'Well, that will give you some time to get things in pristine order, won't it, Clarissa?' Aunt Violet looked at her niece. 'We'd want the house looking her best. And perhaps, Clementine, you can convince Mrs Mogg to make me something new to wear. I'd like to look my best too.'

'Are you in possession of a time machine, Miss Appleby?' Digby Pertwhistle gave the woman a wry smile.

'Very funny, Pertwhistle.'

The adults around the table did their best to smother smiles.

'Why does Aunt Violet need a time machine, Uncle Digby?' Clementine asked.

'I don't. Pertwhistle just wanted to borrow it so he could travel back and locate his hair,' the old woman quipped.

This time everyone laughed out loud. Even Uncle Digby.

THE ATTIC

Clementine and the children soon finished their afternoon tea and began fidgeting in their seats.

'Mummy, may we go up to my room?' Clementine asked. She was keen to show her new friends around the house, just as the children had shown her their home the day before.

Lady Clarissa nodded. 'Yes, of course, darling. I'm going to give Basil and Ana a tour in a little while.'

'I could do that,' Aunt Violet offered. 'Wouldn't you prefer to get on with the washing up?'

Clarissa glared at her aunt. 'No, Aunt Violet. The washing up can wait. But you're welcome to join us if you'd like.'

The old woman's mouth puckered.

Uncle Digby offered everyone some more tea.

'See you later,' Clementine said.

She darted away and the three Hobbs children followed her up the back stairs to the landing.

'What's up here?' Araminta asked.

'This is where the guests stay.' Clementine said. 'My room's on the next floor.'

She raced up the second flight of steps and along the corridor. Clemmie's room was at the front of the house, overlooking the garden. It was a large space with high ceilings and a pretty bedstead. She had a beautiful old rocking horse, which had been in the family longer than anyone could remember, and a doll's house that Aunt Violet said had been given to her as a child.

'What a lovely room,' Araminta said.

'This used to be Aunt Violet's bedroom when she was a little girl,' Clementine explained.

Teddy climbed up on the rocking horse and Araminta and Tilda explored the doll's house. After a few minutes, Clementine offered to show them the rest of the house.

The group followed Clementine back into the corridor, where she pointed out the bedrooms belonging to Uncle Digby, her mother and Aunt Violet.

Araminta looked towards a little door at the end of the hall. 'What's through there?' she asked.

'The stairs to the attic,' said Clementine.

'The attic?' Teddy's face lit up. 'What's up there?'

'Lots of stuff. Do you want to see it?'

'Yes, please,' the twins chorused.

Clementine opened the door and walked into a small corridor with a staircase. She flicked on the light.

Araminta hung back a bit. 'Is it dark?'

'No.' Clementine shook her head. 'But there's lots of junk.'

Teddy looked at Tilda and winked. 'I don't know. It looks pretty dark to me. And spooky. Don't you think, Mintie?'

Araminta frowned.

'Don't look so scared, Mintie. If there are any ghosts Teddy and I will protect you.' Tilda grabbed hold of her big sister's hand.

Araminta didn't want to believe in ghosts, but if they were ever going to see one, surely it would be in the attic of a grand old house like this. She hated that her little brother and sister were so much braver than she was.

Clemmie led the way. 'Wow!' she exclaimed. 'I can't see sunlight through the slates any more.'

But her visitors weren't remotely interested in the newly repaired roof.

They reached the top and Clementine flicked on another light switch.

The three visitors couldn't believe all of the

things that were jammed into the enormous space.

'Look at this.' Teddy ran over to a large dome, which contained a stuffed pheasant.

One side of the room was taken up by a row of old wardrobes.

'What's in those?' Araminta asked hesitantly.

'Dress-ups,' Clementine said. She guessed what was troubling the older girl. 'No ghosts.'

Clementine opened the closest wardrobe and pulled out a long ball gown. It was pink and had faded flowers around the neckline.

Araminta and the twins gasped as they realised that the whole wardrobe was crammed with clothes, and so was the next one and the one after that.

'That one there has hats,' Clementine said and scurried over to open it. She pulled out a black bonnet and popped it on her head.

'That's so cute,' Tilda giggled.

As well as the wardrobes, there was all manner of furniture, knick-knacks and household items.

'Look at this vacuum!' Teddy exclaimed. He picked up the handle. 'It looks like a spaceship.'

'What about this?' Tilda had pushed her way further into the room and located a gigantic globe of the world on a timber stand.

'There's a better one in the library,' Clementine said.

All of a sudden Araminta squealed.

'What's the matter?' Clementine called.

'Did you find a ghost?' her little brother teased.

Araminta hesitated. 'There's ... there's a ... creature ...'

Clementine knew at once what the girl was looking at. 'No, that's just Theodore. He won't hurt you.'

'Are you sure?' Araminta squeaked. 'He looks real to me.'

Clementine closed the wardrobe door and hurried over to the girl. Tilda and Teddy followed her.

'Wow,' Teddy laughed.

'Hello Theo,' Clementine cooed. 'This is Mintie and the twins, Teddy and Tilda.' Before her was a stuffed warthog complete with tusks.

'Where did it come from?' Tilda asked, a look of horror on her face.

'Great Grandpa Appleby went on a safari to Africa a long time ago. Theo used to live in the library but Mummy said that he upset too many of the guests, so now he has to live up here.'

Araminta gulped. 'Are there any more creatures?'

'No.' Clementine shook her head. 'Mummy gave Boo to a museum. He was a lion.'

'I think it's awful how in the olden days people used to shoot wild animals just so they could have them stuffed and put in the lounge room,' said Araminta.

'That's what Mummy and Uncle Digby said too. Uncle Digby said that people weren't as smart about animals back then and they didn't realise they could become stink,' Clementine explained.

'Do you mean "extinct", Clementine?' Araminta asked with a smile.

'Oh.' Clementine giggled. 'That's what I meant.'

The children continued their explorations until they heard Lady Clarissa's voice.

'Clementine, are you up there?'

'Yes, Mummy,' Clemmie called back.

There was the sound of footsteps on the stairs and Lady Clarissa appeared at the end of the room.

'Goodness me, darling, I'm so pleased that you're showing off the most beautiful parts of the house.' Lady Clarissa shook her head. 'Have you taken the children to see the library and the sitting room?'

'Not yet,' Clementine said. 'We were going there next.'

Tilda's head popped up. She was wearing a striking pink hat with a long peacock feather sticking out of the top. Teddy had found himself an old triangular hat, which looked like it was from a navy uniform.

The girl grinned. 'It's fun up here.'

'Yeah, it's way more exciting than our attic,' Teddy added.

'I just think it's an awful mess. One of these days we're going to have to sort it out,' Lady Clarissa replied with a smile. 'I'm glad you're having fun, but I have to interrupt it. We're all going to walk over to the village. Mrs Mogg called to say there's a meeting at the church to talk about the hall.'

Tilda and Teddy put their hats back into the wardrobe and the children made their way through the maze of bric-a-brac to Lady Clarissa.

'Is Aunt Violet coming, Mummy?' Clementine asked.

'Yes, I think she's having a lovely time with Ana and Basil,' Lady Clarissa replied.

Her aunt was being far more hospitable than usual. Clarissa had a sneaking suspicion that it had more to do with Ana being a famous ballerina than anything else.

'Can we take Lavender?'

'Yes, she needs a walk. Why don't you run along and get her ready. I'll take the children downstairs and show them the library and the sitting room and we'll meet you at the front door in a few minutes.'

Clementine nodded and scurried off.

The Hobbs children followed Lady Clarissa.

A few minutes later, the Hobbses and Applebys gathered out the front of Penberthy House.

'It's really a splendid house, Clarissa,' Basil enthused.

'Thank you, Basil. We love her, even though she's a bit worn around the edges.' Lady Clarissa smiled.

'So you'll think about the film then?' Basil's eyes twinkled.

Lady Clarissa nodded.

Aunt Violet tutted. 'Really, Clarissa, you should give Basil the go-ahead right away.'

'I'm a little surprised by your enthusiasm, Aunt Violet,' said Clarissa. 'When you realised that I'd opened the hotel you were less than impressed about sharing Penberthy House with anyone.'

'Well, that was different. Basil's team won't be nearly as invasive,' said Aunt Violet.

'I'm afraid we will be,' Basil said earnestly. 'The crew will have to stay here while we're filming, and I'll be doing lots of research to uncover everything I possibly can about the house and the family.'

'So you'll have to find out why Aunt Violet came to live with us,' Clementine said.

Aunt Violet's jaw dropped. 'That's quite enough, Clementine. My living here is of no interest to anyone.'

'I'm afraid you're wrong about that,' Basil said, rubbing his beard. 'People love a human interest story.'

'Yes, well, we'll need some more time to think about things won't we, Clarissa?' Aunt Violet glared at her niece, who could barely contain a smile. The old woman stalked off down the driveway. Basil frowned at Ana in puzzlement, wondering what Aunt Violet was hiding.

'Do you want to hold Lavender's lead?' Clementine asked Teddy.

'Yes, please,' the boy said.

'That pig is so cute,' said Araminta, as she and her younger sister walked along behind.

Lavender turned and gave a little grunt just as Araminta spoke.

'She always knows when someone is talking about her,' Clementine said with a smile.

VILLAGE MEETING

There were at least as many people in the village that afternoon as there had been the night before. But this time they weren't wearing dressing-gowns.

Father Bob was standing at the church gate welcoming everyone. Lady Clarissa introduced the Hobbses and then the group followed some of the other village residents inside. Mr and Mrs Mogg were sitting down the front and Joshua Tribble and his parents and older brother were on the other side of the church.

After a moment, Father Bob bustled down the aisle. 'Good afternoon, everyone,' he said. 'Thank you all for coming at such short notice. I've spoken to Commander Sprout of the Highton Mill fire brigade. Today the brigade conducted a thorough investigation and it seems that the fire was indeed caused by faulty electrical wiring.'

Margaret Mogg gasped.

'Please don't worry yourself, Margaret. It had nothing to do with you turning off the lights. The brigade believe the fire started long after that.'

A murmur went around the church. The villagers were glad to hear there had been no foul play involved and Mrs Mogg was relieved to know that she hadn't caused the fire.

'Now, as you've all seen, there's not much left of the old hall and what remains will have to be demolished. I'd like to thank you all for your support last night and I'd particularly like to thank Digby Pertwhistle and Clementine Appleby, who first noticed the fire.'

Uncle Digby was sitting beside Clemmie and gave her a nudge and a wink. Clementine's face felt as if it were burning a little bit.

Father Bob beamed at her and then looked around the church hall. 'Before I get to the most pressing business of the day, I would like to welcome our newest residents, Mr and Mrs Hobbs and their three children, to the village. We're always pleased to have new folk in town and I hope that you'll enjoy living here.'

Basil and Ana smiled. Clementine noticed some of the villagers craning their necks to take a look.

'Thank you, Father Bob,' Basil said. 'I'm sure that we are going to love Penberthy Floss.'

Father Bob nodded at him. 'Now, we need to work out how we are going to rebuild the hall. It seems that the insurance won't cover the full cost. Unless there is a builder willing to work for sandwiches and cake among you, I think we're going to have to put our thinking caps on and come up with some fundraising ideas.'

People began chatting at once.

'We could have a pet day,' Clementine called out. 'We had one at school to raise money for Queen Georgiana's Animals.'

Father Bob smiled at the child. 'Very good, Clementine. That's not a bad idea at all.'

'What about a fair?' said Mrs Mogg.

'Yes, we could have a fair but it might take a little while to organise,' Father Bob replied. 'Is there something we could do quickly?'

Basil leaned over and whispered in Lady Clarissa's ear. She turned to him and smiled. 'That's a great idea, Basil. If you think people would come?'

'Absolutely,' he said.

'What about we open Penberthy House and the garden and charge visitors a fee for a guided tour?' Lady Clarissa said.

There was a murmur of approval around the room. Aunt Violet glared at Lady Clarissa.

Mrs Tribble raised her hand.

'Yes?' Father Bob looked at the woman. He hoped her suggestion was sensible, given that she looked as if she might cry if it wasn't well received.

'What about a jumble sale on the lawn at Penberthy House at the same time?' she said.

'Oh, godfathers no,' Aunt Violet moaned. 'I don't think we want a whole lot of other people's junk masking the beauty of our home.'

Mrs Tribble's lip began to tremble.

'I don't know, Miss Appleby. I think that's rather a good idea. Surely we all have some bits and pieces at home that we'd like to clear out,' said Father Bob. He gave Mrs Tribble a wink.

'You're not getting rid of my toys,' Joshua whined. His father glared at him.

'What if we have a cake stall at the same time?' Mrs Mogg suggested. 'I'm sure Pierre Rousseau would be willing to lend a hand.'

'It could be like a mini fete,' Clyde Mogg said. 'Instead of a pet show, Clementine, perhaps people might pay to have their picture taken with your Lavender?'

Clementine's eyes lit up.

'We should take a vote,' said Father Bob.

Heads nodded all over the church.

'Who would like to support a fete hosted in the grounds of Penberthy House?'

Hands shot into the air.

Father Bob glanced around and noticed only one person without a raised hand – both of hers were firmly clasped in her lap.

'Miss Appleby, do you have a better idea?' the man asked.

Ana Hobbs turned to Lady Clarissa and whispered loudly, 'What wonderful community spirit. I'm so glad we moved here.'

Aunt Violet heard her and gulped.

'Well, Miss Appleby, is there something else you think we should do instead?' Father Bob asked.

Aunt Violet's hand crept upwards and she gave an ever-so-slight shake of her head.

'Splendid,' the man said. 'It's unanimous. Now, shall we set a date?'

It was quickly decided to hold the fete the weekend after next. Mrs Mogg was put in charge of the cake stall. Mrs Tribble would coordinate the jumble sale as long as donations could be taken straight to Penberthy House. Uncle Digby agreed to help her. They could store items in the old garden shed. Basil said that he'd be happy to contact the local newspapers.

Clementine was very excited about setting up a photo booth with Lavender. Araminta and the twins offered to help. Ana offered to paint signs and put them up around the village and some of the surrounding villages too.

'What about you, Aunt Violet?' Clementine turned and looked at her great-aunt. 'What are you going to do to help?'

The old woman thought for a moment. 'Supervise.'

'Aunt Violet, why don't you coordinate the tours of the house?' Lady Clarissa asked. 'You know the place better than anyone.'

87

Aunt Violet straightened her back. 'Yes, I suppose that's true. And then I could make sure that people don't go anywhere we don't want them.'

Lady Clarissa looked at Clementine and gave a sly smile. 'Of course,' she said.

PLANS

The villagers spilled out of the church into the sunshine. Clementine, Araminta and the twins took Lavender for a walk around the garden while the adults chatted.

'I'm so excited about the fete,' Araminta said. 'But I don't think we've got anything much for the jumble sale.'

Clementine's face lit up. 'We have heaps,' she said. 'In the attic.'

'Of course,' Tilda said. 'There's loads of stuff up there.'

'Me and Tilda can help you sort it out,' Teddy said.

'I can too,' Araminta added. She didn't want the little kids to think she was a complete scaredy-cat.

'Can you hold Lavender for a minute?' Clementine passed the little pig's lead to Tilda and ran over to where her mother, Uncle Digby and Mrs Mogg were busy discussing the best position for the cake stall.

'Mummy,' Clementine called, interrupting the threesome.

'Clementine,' her mother looked at her with a frown. 'What do you need to remember?'

Clementine bit her lip. 'Excuse me, Mummy.'

'That's better,' said Lady Clarissa.

'Mummy, can we have a clear-out for the jumble sale?' Clementine was bouncing about with excitement.

'Yes, of course. Do you have some toys you'd like to donate?'

Clementine thought for a moment. 'Maybe. But I meant in the attic.'

Lady Clarissa nodded. 'That's a wonderful idea, Clementine. I can't believe I didn't think of it.'

'We can finally get rid of some junk,' Uncle Digby chimed in. 'And then we'll have room to take some more junk up there.'

Clementine giggled. 'Can Mintie and the twins help me? We can sort it all out.'

'If it's all right with Basil and Ana, yes, absolutely. But there's a lot,' Clarissa said. 'It might take a while.'

'And not all of it's worthless, my dear,' said Uncle Digby. 'I think you'll find some treasures.'

Clarissa nodded. 'I could send the really valuable things off to auction and we can add that money to the fund for the hall too.'

Aunt Violet approached the group at that moment. 'What auction?' she asked.

Clarissa explained.

'And what exactly are you planning to do with the money?' Aunt Violet asked.

'Mummy said that we can donate it for the hall,' Clementine said.

'I don't think so,' Aunt Violet protested. 'You should be using it to fix that wretched bathroom I have to share.'

'We'll see about that,' Clarissa said firmly. She turned to her daughter. 'Clemmie, would you rather have a new bath or ballet lessons?'

Clementine's eyes lit up. 'That's easy, Mummy. I want to do ballet. In a red tutu.'

'Of course *you'd* want that,' Aunt Violet said with a sneer. 'I'd much rather have a bath without scratching my bottom.'

Digby Pertwhistle and Mrs Mogg smiled at one another.

'What are you smiling about, Pertwhistle? Your bath is fine. And you don't have to share it either,' Aunt Violet grumbled.

'Thank goodness for that, Miss Appleby. I can't imagine sharing a bath with you,' said Uncle Digby. He winked at Mrs Mogg.

'Digby Pertwhistle, you cheeky thing,' Mrs Mogg laughed. 'Oh well, I'd best get over to the shop.'

'Bye, Mrs Mogg,' Clementine called.

'Bye bye, dear,' said the old woman, waving.

Lady Clarissa looked at her watch. 'It's time for us to get home too. We've got guests arriving in an hour. Clementine, we won't be able to start any sorting until Sunday afternoon, when the weekend rush is over.'

'Heavens, I'd almost forgotten,' Uncle Digby said. 'But I think the house is in order.' He frowned at Clementine, raising his eyebrows. She had a habit of leaving things in the most inopportune places.

'It's okay, Uncle Digby. We played in my bedroom and the attic. I promise there are no surprises anywhere.'

Digby grinned at her.

Basil and Ana had met just about everyone in the village by now. Basil wandered over and Ana rounded up the children, who joined the group.

Tilda still had hold of Lavender's lead. The little pig was nibbling on a violet in the garden bed by the path.

'Mummy said that we can clear out some

of the things in the attic for the jumble sale,' Clementine informed her friends. 'Can you come on Sunday?'

The Hobbs children excitedly explained the plan to their parents, who thought it was a great idea. But they wouldn't be able to help until early the next week. They were off on Sunday for a couple of days in the city to celebrate their grandmother's birthday.

'When we finish unpacking, Basil can bring up some moving boxes. We've certainly got enough of them,' Ana offered.

'That would be wonderful,' said Lady Clarissa.

'I'll get a start on the signs tomorrow. The children can help me and perhaps Clementine would like to come down for the morning?' Ana said.

'Yes, please,' Clementine said.

The children skipped along in front of their parents, buzzing about the fete.

THINGS THAT GO BUMP . . .

Clementine was out collecting the mail with Uncle Digby when Basil Hobbs delivered a car load of packing boxes to Penberthy House the following week. Clementine and the children had painted the signs with Ana the day after the meeting and Basil had put them up all around the village and in Highton Mill too. But then the children had gone away and Penberthy House had been busy with more guests. Clementine couldn't wait to see Tilda and Teddy and Araminta again and to start sorting the attic.

Basil balanced several boxes and followed Lady Clarissa upstairs. When he saw the treasure trove in the attic, he was tempted to stay and help.

'Clarissa, if you don't mind me saying, please make sure that you check the children's decisions on what can go into the jumble sale,' the man said as he spied a stunning Tiffany lamp on top of a mahogany side table.

'Yes, I certainly will, Basil. I thought that they could be in charge of the more ordinary household items.' Lady Clarissa picked up a cracked pie plate. 'Like this. Uncle Digby and I will look after everything else.'

Basil wandered to the other end of the room. 'Oh my heavens, where did you get him?'

'I presume you've found Theo.' Lady Clarissa edged through the furniture to join the man. 'He's very handsome, don't you think?'

'He'd scare the socks off anyone,' Basil grinned.

'That's why he's up here. He was in the library until one of our guests took a walk in the middle of the night. The poor woman screamed so loudly I thought there must have been an intruder. When I found her she was as white as a sheet and frozen to the spot, demanding that I call the police and have the animal shot. I didn't have the heart to tell her that my grandfather had already done that about eighty years earlier. The next day Uncle Digby and I heaved and hefted Theo up here. You know, he's awful but I just can't bear to part with him. He's been in the family for such a long time.'

'He'd have to be sent to auction anyway, Clarissa. There must be collectors who delight in that sort of thing. It's not my cup of tea but someone would love him,' Basil said as he cast his eyes over the rest of the bric-a-brac. 'I should get going. The children couldn't fit in the car with me and all the boxes but they'll be up soon.'

Lady Clarissa had just farewelled Basil and was on her way to the kitchen when she heard the back door slam.

'Are they here yet?' Clementine called as she almost bumped into her mother. She'd been bursting to see the Hobbs children again for days.

'Hello darling, did you have a good walk?'

Clementine nodded.

The doorbell rang.

'They're here!' Clementine raced into the hall and skidded along the polished timber floorboards in her socks. She wrenched open the front door.

'Hello,' Clementine said.

'Hi,' the twins chorused.

'Hello,' Araminta said.

Lady Clarissa walked up behind Clementine. 'Good morning. Your father dropped off the boxes a few minutes ago. Come in.'

'How was your grandmother's birthday celebration?' Lady Clarissa asked.

'It was fun. Granny had a huge cake and it had about a hundred candles on it,' Tilda said.

'It was only eighty, Tilda,' said Araminta, shaking her head.

'That's even more than Aunt Violet,' Clementine said. She couldn't imagine that many people in the world were older than her. 'Can we go upstairs, Mummy?'

Lady Clarissa nodded. 'I think I might help for a little while. There's a lot to get through. And then I have to make some phone calls and do some paperwork.'

Clementine nodded. 'We can do it, Mummy. I promise.'

Lady Clarissa smiled at the eager foursome. 'Come on, then. Let's go and do battle, shall we?'

The children followed Lady Clarissa up to the attic. She had already pulled back the shutters to let in as much light as possible.

'Now, I thought you could find anything that was household related. Like the vacuum, and the pots and pans down the back. There's a huge number of old kitchen utensils, too. Why don't you stack them into boxes and then I can have a look afterwards. Uncle Digby and I will take care of all the decorative things and the furniture and maybe Aunt Violet can help with the clothes.'

'Oh no, Mummy, please don't sell the dress-ups,' Clementine begged.

'You know, Mummy said that when the ballet school is up and running, she'd have a concert at the end of every year. Some of the clothes would be perfect for that,' Araminta said.

Clementine nodded. 'That's a great idea.'

Her mother relented with a smile. 'Okay, Clementine, the clothes can stay. Now, does everyone know what they're looking for?'

'Yes,' the children chorused. Clementine, Tilda and Teddy headed straight to the far end of the attic.

'I think there's an old mixer down here,' Clementine said.

Araminta got started on a huge old dresser full of cutlery and utensils.

Lady Clarissa spent about fifteen minutes watching them. When she was satisfied that they weren't about to put anything especially valuable in the boxes, she headed downstairs.

'Hey, look at this,' Araminta called. Clementine and the twins made their way to the other side of the attic.

'What is it?' Tilda asked.

Clementine looked at the bowl. 'I've seen one of those before,' she said. She suddenly remembered. 'Oh! That's an old-fashioned toilet.'

'Yuck,' said Araminta. She peered inside. 'At least it's clean.'

Teddy looked at it too. 'I wonder how many of your relatives have used that.'

Clementine shrugged. The children continued their sorting and packing and were surprised that they already had six boxes of household items for the stall.

'Does anyone feel like a drink?' Clementine asked.

The children nodded. Araminta wiped some beads of perspiration from her brow. 'I thought you were never going to ask.'

'Let's get some morning tea and come back later,' Clementine said.

Just as they were about to leave, there was a loud thud.

'What was that?' Teddy said.

The children looked to see if anything had fallen over.

'Probably just something in one of the cupboards falling down,' Clementine said confidently. She walked over to the first wardrobe and opened the doors, but everything was still in place. She wandered along and opened each one but couldn't see anything unusual.

There was another thud, this time louder than the first.

Araminta jumped. 'Can we go?' she said, her knees trembling.

'It's all right. I've been up here lots of times,' Clementine said. 'It's probably a mouse.'

Teddy had wandered off into the far corner of the room and discovered a narrow door.

'Clementine, where does this go?' the boy called.

Clementine scampered over with Tilda and Araminta behind her. She couldn't remember seeing the door before. Maybe her mother had moved something out of the way earlier.

'Open it,' she said.

Teddy turned the handle, wondering what he'd find.

It was certainly not what he was expecting.

'Ahhhh!' the twins and Araminta screamed in unison. 'It's a skeleton!'

The three Hobbs children raced off towards the stairs. Clementine giggled. So much for the twins wanting to find a ghost. But Clementine wasn't frightened. She peeked in.

'Hello, who are you?' she said. She was about to leave when she heard a scraping noise. It was loud and didn't sound like any of the mice she'd come across before. She jumped and ran down the attic stairs, along the hall and down

the back stairs to the kitchen. She found her friends all talking at once, telling Lady Clarissa about the thuds and the skeleton in the other room.

'Mummy, I told the children there was nothing up there but when I looked at the skeleton, I heard a scraping noise and I didn't know what it was either. Where did the skeleton come from? Is it someone in the family?' Clementine fired the questions at her mother.

Lady Clarissa directed the children to sit down. She pulled a large pitcher of homemade lemonade out of the fridge and set it down on the table.

'The skeleton's nothing to worry about. I'd forgotten about him actually,' she said. 'He first belonged to your great-grandfather, Clementine. He was a doctor and that skeleton was affectionately known as Claude. We inherited him. Your grandmother used to love playing tricks on your grandfather with him. She'd put him in all sorts of odd places around the house when I was a girl and then wait for your grandpa to bellow. She and I loved it. Uncle Digby used to get in on the act too, I think,' Lady Clarissa explained.

The old man walked into the room balancing a tea tray. He'd just served morning tea to the guests who'd arrived the previous evening.

'What did I do?' he asked, setting the tray on the bench near the sink.

'The children discovered Claude upstairs in the attic,' Lady Clarissa explained. 'Do you remember that time Mummy and I took Claude and set him up in Daddy's office chair in the library? The poor man almost had a heart attack when he spun the chair around and went to sit down.'

'Oh yes, that was funny. But I think the best one was when we put him in the back of your father's car with a hat and a coat. Your father was halfway to Highton Mill before he realised who his passenger was,' Uncle Digby said with a giggle. 'Although that was very silly of us.

In hindsight, the poor man could have had a nasty accident.'

The children listened to the stories and felt much better about the skeleton.

'But that still doesn't explain the thuds and the scraping sound,' Araminta said, frowning.

'It could have been anything,' said Uncle Digby. 'And I might just set a few rat traps in case the builders let some creatures in while the roof was being done.'

'Was it Lavender?' Lady Clarissa asked. 'Or Pharaoh?' Both animals were missing from their usual spot in Lavender's basket.

Clementine shook her head. 'I didn't see either of them up there and usually Pharaoh meows so loudly to let you know he's around.'

'I wonder if it really could be a ghost,' Tilda said. 'Daddy says that all old houses have ghosts.'

Araminta flinched. 'I don't want to go up there again.'

'I've lived here all my life and I've never seen any ghosts. Why don't you go and play in the garden for a little while and get some fresh air,' Lady Clarissa suggested. 'You can do some more sorting later, if you like.'

While the attic was a treasure trove, outside the sun was shining and the skeleton had put the visitors off going back upstairs for now.

'Do you want to play hide-and-seek?' Clementine asked.

'Okay,' Tilda and Teddy said at the same time.

Araminta nodded.

Lady Clarissa set a plate of chocolate-chip biscuits on the table.

'Why don't you take these into the garden,' she said. 'I'll see if I can find Lavender and Pharaoh and shoo them out.'

Before she could move, a squeal came from the sitting room.

'Oh, oh, what on earth?' a woman called loudly. 'Good gracious, there's a monster in here.'

'Oops! I think our guests have just met Pharaoh.' Lady Clarissa dashed off.

Clementine giggled and the others did too.

GONE IN A FLASH

Clementine and her friends played hide-and-seek, followed by chasings, stuck in the mud and a rowdy game of soccer. Teddy and Tilda said that they were eager to join Clementine's Saturday team if there was room for a couple more players. Clementine thought that was a great idea.

Lady Clarissa had rescued Pharaoh from the startled guests and quickly located Lavender. The pair were sent outside with the children. Lavender couldn't decide which side she was on, chasing the ball in both directions. Pharaoh wasn't remotely interested. He jumped up on one of the outdoor chairs and promptly fell asleep.

Uncle Digby made the children some sandwiches and they ate lunch outside. Ana arrived soon afterwards.

She walked onto the back steps with Lady Clarissa. 'Hello everyone, how's the attic sorting?'

'We got six boxes done, but then Mintie got scared,' Teddy said.

Araminta glared at her brother. 'It wasn't just me. You and Tilda ran away too.'

'I hope you've been helpful,' Ana said. 'Anyway, I'm sorry, kids, but we have to get going. I almost forgot that you're all having haircuts this afternoon in Highton Mill.'

Clementine and her mother watched and waved as the Hobbses' car drove out the driveway.

'Now, why don't you and I do some more sorting,' Lady Clarissa suggested. 'Uncle Digby said he has a bit of time now too. The guests have gone for a long drive and won't be back until dinnertime.'

'Okay, Mummy,' Clementine said, and the two walked upstairs. She wasn't scared about being up there with her mother and Uncle Digby.

Digby Pertwhistle had already pulled out an interesting array of lamps, ornaments and statues. He was waiting for Clarissa to help move some of the larger pieces.

'Goodness, what have you found, Uncle Digby?' Clarissa asked as she surveyed the items.

'Oh, this and that. But there's lots more.'

'What do you want me to do, Mummy?' Clementine asked.

'Hmm, why don't you see what's in the dresser in the back corner.'

Clementine scurried off, saying hello to Theodore on her way. She opened the dresser drawers and found a whole set of knives and forks and spoons. Clementine dumped them into a box that one of the twins had moved to the far end of the attic.

She opened the dresser doors and found three different-sized wooden boxes.

'Mummy, what are these?' she called.

Lady Clarissa made her way over.

'Oh, they're music boxes. The smallest one was mine when I was little. I kept all my precious things inside. I'd forgotten about it. I don't know where the others came from.'

Lady Clarissa pulled out the box that belonged to her. She opened the lid and a beautiful ballerina sprang up on a platform.

Clementine gasped. 'Does she dance?'

Her mother turned the box around and found a little winder. She gave it a crank and put the box on the dresser. Music began to play and the tiny dancer started to twirl.

'Mummy, she's lovely,' Clementine said. 'Can I keep her?'

Lady Clarissa nodded. She reached in and pulled out a slightly larger box. This time when

she lifted the lid, the ballerina was broken and the lining torn.

'I think this one can go out,' she said, and placed it in the box with the cutlery.

The last box was almost twice the size of the others. Inside, the ballerina was tatty and no longer twirled. Clarissa was about to put it in with the goods for the fete when the telephone rang.

'I'll get it, Clarissa,' Digby called from the other end of the room.

'No, don't you run. I'll go.' Clarissa put the music box on the floor and dashed as quickly as she could to the telephone in the hall on the third floor. She didn't like the old man rushing. A health scare earlier in the year had landed him in hospital and given them all a nasty fright.

Clementine stared at her twirling ballerina. When the music stopped she wound the spring again and again, listening to the same tune chiming over and over.

Her mother returned and began to help Uncle Digby move several side tables.

'Clemmie, why don't you take that and show Aunt Violet,' she suggested.

'Okay, Mummy.'

Uncle Digby grinned. 'Thank you, Clarissa,' he whispered. 'I don't think I want to hear that tune ever again.'

Clementine didn't see the little creature crawl its way into the largest box, which her mother had left sitting open on the floor. And over the din of the chimes, she didn't hear the scraping noise that had startled her earlier. Clementine picked up her new treasure and spun around, almost tripping over the box on the floor. She kicked the lid with her foot and it snapped shut.

Clementine put her precious music box on the dresser and picked up the other one from the floor. 'You're supposed to be in there.' She deposited it into the cardboard box for the fete.

'See you later,' she said to her mother and Uncle Digby as she sped downstairs to find Aunt Violet.

'You know your aunt won't thank you for sending Clementine in her direction,' Uncle Digby smiled.

Lady Clarissa grinned. 'No, I'm sure to hear about it later, although I think we might have sent Clemmie on a wild goose chase. I've just remembered that Aunt Violet's gone to visit Mrs Bottomley. Let's just get this done and we can go and have a cup of tea.'

FETE DAY

Clementine woke up just as the clock in the hall struck seven. She rushed to the window. The afternoon before, some men had put up a stripy blue marquee on the front lawn for Mrs Mogg's cafe. In the dim morning light, Clementine could see Father Bob and Mr Mogg moving trestle tables with Mrs Tribble directing them.

Clementine ran to the wardrobe and pulled out her favourite red dress and matching shoes. She quickly got dressed and brushed her hair, pinning it back with a red bow.

Lavender was making snuffly grunts in her basket at the end of the bed. Clementine decided to let the little pig sleep. She needed her to look her best for the photographs.

Clementine, Araminta and the twins had spent the previous afternoon finding the perfect backdrop for Lavender's photo booth. They had tossed up between the rose garden out the front and the fountain around the back of the house. It was Lady Clarissa who decided that it would be better for business if they stayed close to the stalls in the front garden. Basil was going to be the photographer for the day.

Clementine was worried about her new friends. A few days before, Flash had gone missing from the Hobbses' house and, although the children had searched high and low, there was no sign of him. Clementine remembered how worried she'd been when Lavender had escaped at the seaside. Tilda was especially upset.

'I'll come back and get you ready after breakfast,' Clementine whispered to Lavender, and then raced into the hallway.

Aunt Violet was walking towards her, carrying a thick plait of red rope and a box of pins.

'You look nice, Aunt Violet.' Clementine admired the woman's smart navy pants-suit and spotty silk blouse. 'What are you doing?'

'I'm roping off all the areas of the house where we don't want people to go.'

Clementine looked down the hallway. The rope was across the top of the main stairs. She took a few steps further and noticed that there was another rope blocking off the floor below. She wondered if the people were going to get any further than the front hall.

'Now run along, Clementine, and don't touch any of my ropes,' Aunt Violet directed.

The kitchen was buzzing. People were coming in and out of the back door, bringing all sorts of delicious treats, and Mrs Tribble was now directing her husband and Mr Mogg as they moved the last of the boxes from the Penberthy House attic.

Mrs Mogg turned from where she was arranging chocolate brownies on a plate. 'Good morning, Clementine. Don't you look lovely.'

'I can't wait for the fete.' Clementine shivered with excitement.

She poured herself some cereal, and Mrs Mogg offered to help with the milk. Usually Clementine liked to do things herself but this morning she didn't want to spill anything on the table or her dress.

Aunt Violet stormed into the kitchen. Her face was red and Clementine could almost see the steam coming out of her ears. 'Who took the rope from the bottom of the staircase?'

Lady Clarissa came down the back stairs at that moment. 'I did, Aunt Violet. You've got hours until the tours begin and I needed to bring some more things downstairs for the jumble sale.'

'What do you call those?' Aunt Violet pointed at the back stairs.

'Aunt Violet, I was trying to take the shortest route to the front garden. Those boxes are heavy, you know.'

'Don't get snippy with me, Clarissa. I've got a lot to do. If you want these tours to work, I simply can't have people traipsing all through the house. There . . . there are rules!' She turned on her heel and strode from the room.

'Her rules,' Uncle Digby muttered.

Clementine finished her breakfast and raced upstairs to get Lavender ready. She was going to wear her best sparkly red collar with the matching lead.

By nine o'clock the stalls were set up, Mrs Mogg's cafe was ready and Aunt Violet had finished roping off the house. As far as Clementine could tell, guests would be allowed in the sitting room, dining room, conservatory and library. Everywhere else was off limits.

Clementine recognised lots of things on Mrs Tribble's bric-a-brac tables but there was loads more that other people in the village had donated too.

Basil and Ana arrived with the children in tow. Clementine and Lavender raced out to greet them.

'Hello,' Clementine said. 'Lavender's all ready for the photos.'

Basil grinned. 'And might I say she looks especially gorgeous today.'

'I'd better get going and help Mrs Tribble,' Ana said.

'Have you found Flash?' Clementine asked.

Tilda shook her head. 'I don't think he's ever coming back.'

'He might have walked home to our old house,' Araminta said. 'I've heard stories of cats and dogs who do that.'

'Then he'll be there in about ten years' time,' Teddy said. 'He's not exactly fast, is he?'

'Stop saying that,' Tilda said sulkily. 'You don't care about him.'

'Yes, I do,' Teddy said. 'He's my tortoise too.'

'But you don't look after him as much as I do.' Tilda's eyes glistened.

'Sorry, Tilda.' Teddy put his arm around his twin sister. 'I'm sure he'll come home.' Teddy wasn't sure at all, but at least if Flash had escaped outside he had a nice place to live by the creek with plenty of things to eat.

'Why don't you go and get your booth ready?' Basil suggested. 'Have you got the money tin and some change sorted?'

Soon the crowds began to pour into the garden. Aunt Violet insisted that she wasn't taking any tours until ten o'clock but by nine-thirty there was a line of people waiting to go in. Mrs Bottomley had come along to help her, so after quite a bit of discussion Aunt Violet decided to open early. She had thought about upping the price for the inconvenience but Mrs Bottomley talked her out of it.

Clementine and her friends were doing great business in their photo booth.

Lavender was behaving perfectly, sitting beside the eager children and adults while Basil snapped away. Tilda and Teddy were taking people's names and telling them what time they could come and collect their pictures, while Araminta was in charge of the money. Clementine made sure that Lavender was feeling all right and not too tired.

By early afternoon the children were starving and Basil said that they should shut up shop for a while and take a break. 'Besides,' he said, 'Lavender has been smiling so much her face must be sore.'

'Lavender can't smile,' Clementine said with a giggle.

Basil winked. 'I don't know, Clementine. I think she can.'

There was a jumping castle that the children had their eyes on and a lucky dip stall that they wanted to visit.

Aunt Violet decided that she and Mrs Bottomley were due for a break too.

Mrs Bottomley was keen to have a quick look at the stalls before the best things were gone.

The crowds had thinned out a bit since the morning rush but Lady Clarissa couldn't believe how much they had already raised.

'What a wonderful day, Clarissa,' Father Bob said as he walked into the kitchen to hand over another tin of money from his flower stall. 'I think we'll have that new hall built sooner than we thought.'

Clarissa smiled. She certainly hoped so.

TREASURE

Clementine and her friends wandered into Mrs Mogg's cafe.

'Hello there, my lovelies. What can I get you?' the woman called.

'May I please have a vanilla milkshake and a chocolate brownie?' Clementine asked. 'And a bowl of water for Lavender, please.'

The other children all ordered chocolate milkshakes and a variety of cupcakes.

Clementine reached into her pocket and

handed over a crisp note. 'It's my pocket money,' she said proudly.

Araminta paid for herself and the twins and the children sat down. Clementine got the water bowl for Lavender and Mrs Mogg gave the little pig an extra brownie. She said it had fallen on the ground earlier and she was saving it especially for her.

Aunt Violet and Mrs Bottomley walked into the tent.

'Hello Aunt Violet. How are your tours going?' Clementine asked.

'Perfectly well, apart from that little monster Joshua Tribble. I found him in my bedroom teasing Pharaoh,' her great-aunt replied. 'But Mrs Bottomley dealt with him. I don't think he'll be trespassing anywhere ever again.'

Mrs Bottomley smiled, revealing a row of yellowed teeth. Clementine wondered what she'd done to him. She didn't like to think. Maybe she'd find Joshua in a cupboard later.

'Who's that?' Tilda whispered as the two women sat down at a nearby table.

'That's Mrs Bottomley. She was my teacher and now she's friends with Aunt Violet,' Clementine whispered back. 'I hope she's not our teacher this year.'

'I heard that, Clementine,' Mrs Bottomley snapped. 'And you'll be pleased to know that I have no intention of taking that class of yours ever again.'

Clementine's eyes widened. 'Yes!' she mouthed.

'Heard that too!' the woman barked.

The children giggled. They finished their treats and decided to take a wander around the stalls. Teddy suggested they go straight to the jumping castle but Araminta, sensible as always, said that they should probably let their afternoon tea go down for a while. She remembered when her brother and sister had ridden a merry-go-round at a fair right after lunch. The results hadn't been pretty.

Teddy and Tilda remembered too and decided to take their big sister's advice.

As well as Mrs Tribble's bric-a-brac and Father Bob's flowers, there was a man selling homemade cheese (which Clementine decided smelt like old socks), another lady had handcrafted baby clothes, and there was a pointy-looking fellow selling paintings. Mr Mogg had a wonderful vegetable stall with home-grown produce, too.

Clementine and her friends were hoping that there was something they could spend their pocket money on. 'What about the lucky dip?' Clementine suggested.

Over in Mrs Mogg's tent, Mrs Bottomley and Aunt Violet finished their tea and decided to take a walk too.

'What a lot of old tat,' Aunt Violet sneered at the cracked plates and chipped vases on Mrs Tribble's stall.

Ethel Bottomley had been admiring a very pretty teapot with a small chip on the rim but put it back down when she heard Aunt Violet's comment. She wandered further along and came to a lovely timber box.

'Oh, this is sweet. I could use that in the classroom for something.' She picked it up and examined the silky timber. 'How much is this one?'

Mrs Tribble looked at the box. She'd sold another smaller one earlier but couldn't remember the price.

'If you give me a moment I'll check.' She ran her finger down the list she'd been keeping of the sales.

Aunt Violet walked up beside Mrs Bottomley. She shook her head. 'Goodness, Ethel, what do you want that old rubbish for?'

'I thought it could come in handy for something. It's pretty, or at least it was once. There are always little bits and pieces – you know, blocks and the like – that I need containers for at school.'

Aunt Violet looked at the box more closely. Suddenly her memory flashed. She gasped.

'No, Ethel, you can't have it,' Aunt Violet said, reaching out to snatch it from her.

Mrs Bottomley clutched the box to her

ample chest. 'What are you doing, Violet? I want it and I'll have it.'

'No! You can't. It's not right for you. It won't go with the classroom decor!' Aunt Violet grabbed at the box.

By now the two women were attracting quite a bit of attention. Clementine looked up from where she was standing further along the row of trestle tables.

'What's Aunt Violet doing?' she asked, wrinkling her nose. 'Come on.' She motioned for her friends to follow.

Lady Clarissa walked out the front door and was horrified to see her aunt and Mrs Bottomley having an almighty tug of war. She raced over and stood in front of them.

'What are you two doing?'

'She can't have this,' gasped Aunt Violet. She was pulling as hard as she could. Mrs Bottomley was gripping the item with all her might.

'It's just an old music box from the attic, Aunt Violet. It's broken. If Mrs Bottomley wants it then she should have it,' Lady Clarissa called. She couldn't believe her eyes and neither could anyone else.

'It's not just an old box. It's my box,' Aunt Violet snapped. 'You should have asked me if you could sell it.'

Clementine, Tilda, Teddy and Araminta were standing beside Lady Clarissa, watching the two old women wrestling.

Basil and Ana were there too. Basil raised his camera to his face but Ana put out her hand.

'No, Basil, you can't take a photograph. They'd never forgive you.' Ana tried to stifle the grin that was tickling her lips.

'Give it to me, Ethel!'

'NO! I'm having it!' Mrs Bottomley shouted.

Joshua Tribble had heard the ruckus and come to investigate too. He roared with laughter at the two old women fighting.

'It's mine!' Aunt Violet bellowed and gave one last heave. Mrs Bottomley let go of the box and Aunt Violet went flying backwards, tumbling over Joshua Tribble.

'Cool, I didn't know old ladies could do somersaults,' said the boy. He crashed to the ground just as the box went soaring into the air.

'Noooooo!' Aunt Violet landed with a thud on her bottom.

The box fell to the ground and the lid sprang open.

There was a collective gasp from the crowd.

'Flash!' Tilda raced forward and looked into the box. She lifted the tortoise out.

'Is he all right?' Clementine asked, trying to see if his shell was still in one piece.

The little tortoise poked his head out and looked at the crowd.

'Oh, Tilda, that's wonderful. But how on earth did he get in there?' Ana said with a frown.

'The moving boxes,' Basil said. 'He must have been in one of the boxes I brought over for the attic. Poor old Flash will be starving.'

Aunt Violet was lying on the ground moaning softly.

'Are you all right, Aunt Violet?' Clementine looked down at her great-aunt, who opened her eyes and sat upright.

'No, of course I'm not all right. Ridiculous nonsense,' she spluttered.

Uncle Digby held out his hand to help her up.

Lady Clarissa eyeballed the woman. 'Aunt Violet, you couldn't possibly have known that Tilda's tortoise was in that box. So why did you want it?'

Clementine knelt down on the grass and looked inside the box. She noticed a lump in the lining at the bottom. 'Mummy, there's something in here.'

'Aunt Violet?' Lady Clarissa asked sharply. 'Are you going to tell me what it is?'

'If my memory serves me correctly, Clarissa, I think you'll find the missing Appleby necklace,' Aunt Violet said with a sniff.

There was another gasp from the crowd.

'Why didn't you just say so, Violet?' Mrs Bottomley pursed her lips. 'I would have given it back to you.'

'Because I suspect *someone* would have liked to keep that a secret, wouldn't they?' said Uncle Digby.

Clementine pulled back the lining of the box.

'Mummy, look! It's Granny's necklace from the painting.' Clementine held up the dazzling jewellery. It glinted in the sunshine.

'Oh, it's lovely.' Lady Clarissa took the long strand of diamonds and pearls from the girl. 'It's even more beautiful in real life.'

'It's mine, Clarissa,' Aunt Violet whispered.

Lady Clarissa shook her head.

'Aunt Violet, this was my mother's and before that it was Granny Appleby's and now it belongs to me. I've made a decision about the necklace and the matching earrings and tiara,' Lady Clarissa said. The rest of the set had been found some months beforehand and now resided in the safe in the library.

'What are you going to do?' Aunt Violet demanded.

'These jewels are so beautiful they should be in a museum. I'm never going to wear them and I doubt Clementine will either. But if we sell them, we'll have more than enough money to rebuild the hall and perhaps there'll be some left over to make the repairs on the house,' Lady Clarissa said firmly.

'No! You can't!' Aunt Violet's lip trembled.

'Aunt Violet, please try to think of someone other than yourself. Besides, I thought a new bathroom might be of some interest.'

The old woman sighed.

'Are you sure, Clarissa?' Mrs Mogg asked. 'You don't have to do that.'

'I know I don't. But what would I rather? That we have a priceless collection of unwearable jewels or that Clementine and her friends get to have ballet lessons and you have your quilting group, Maraget, and Father Bob has the flower show.'

'Clarissa, you're a marvel, my dear,' Father Bob declared.

'Don't thank me. Thank Clementine. It was her idea to clean out the attic. We might never have found the necklace otherwise.'

Clementine smiled. 'Will I get to wear a red tutu?'

Mrs Mogg smiled down at her. 'I'll start right away.'

Clementine looked at Tilda and Teddy and Araminta. Flash was nibbling on a piece of lettuce someone had found on the vegetable stall.

The four children grinned at one another.

'It wasn't just an old box after all, was it Mummy?'

'No, Clemmie.' Her mother shook her head. 'It was a box full of treasure.'

CAST OF CHARACTERS

The Appleby household

Clementine Rose Appleby	Five-year-old daughter of Lady Clarissa
Lavender	Clemmie's teacup pig
Lady Clarissa Appleby	Clementine's mother and the owner of Penberthy House
Digby Pertwhistle	Butler at Penberthy House
Aunt Violet Appleby	Clementine's grandfather's sister

Pharaoh	Aunt Violet's beloved sphynx cat

Friends and village folk

Margaret Mogg	Owner of the Penberthy Floss village shop
Father Bob	Village minister
Pierre Rousseau	Owner of Pierre's Patisserie in Highton Mill
Mrs Ethel Bottomley	Teacher at Ellery Prep
Mrs Tribble	Villager and mother of Joshua
Joshua Tribble	Boy in Clementine's class at school
Basil Hobbs	Documentary filmmaker and new neighbour
Ana Hobbs	Former prima ballerina and new neighbour
Araminta Hobbs	Ten-year-old daughter of Basil and Ana

Teddy Hobbs	Five-year-old twin son of Basil and Ana
Tilda Hobbs	Five-year-old twin daughter of Basil and Ana
Flash	Tilda and Teddy's pet tortoise

ABOUT
THE AUTHOR

Jacqueline Harvey taught for many years in girls' boarding schools. She is the author of the bestselling Alice-Miranda series and the Clementine Rose series, and was awarded Honour Book in the 2006 Australian CBC Awards for her picture book *The Sound of the Sea*. She now writes full-time and is working on more Alice-Miranda and Clementine Rose adventures.

www.jacquelineharvey.com.au

JACQUELINE SUPPORTS

Jacqueline Harvey is a passionate educator who enjoys sharing her love of reading and writing with children and adults alike. She is an ambassador for Dymocks Children's Charities and Room to Read. Find out more at www.dcc.gofundraise.com.au and www.roomtoread.org.

Collection One

CLEMENTINE ROSE

3 books in 1

Jacqueline Harvey

OUT NOW